WOUNDED TONGUE

BY GARRETT DENNERT

For information about permission to reproduce selections from this book, write to Orson's Publishing at editor@orsonspublishing.com.

www.orsonspublishing.com

ISBN 978-0-9914463-0-8

This is a work of fiction. Names, characters, businesses, places, events and incidents are either the products of the author's imagination or used in a fictitious manner. Any resemblance to actual persons, living or dead, or actual events is purely coincidental.

For Cecil and Raphael

I.

A note has been stapled to the front door. The size of a playing card. Construction staple through its center, wind-slit edges flapping in the night.

Vitri stands among the weeds that have overthrown his front lawn, squinting through night at the note. Save for unraveling the scarf from his nose and mouth, he does not move. He waits. He listens. For the creak of a car door. For some savage cry. For a piston to fall from any of the gutted SUVs and sedans still along the street, their tires extracted and rolled to alleys, axles flat on asphalt. But there is nothing. No movement whatsoever. No unfamiliar scent, no sound but that of the flapping paper. Each house still stands like his: stripped of its paint, the blues, the reds, the yellows, reduced instead to khaki, to patches of rot and mold. All windows: boarded. All lights: out.

Vitri walks to the front door, eyes not wide but scanning, right hand gripping the 9mm pistol in his waistband as he surmounts the four steps before him and shuffles along his porch. So as not to damage the note, he pries the staple from the door with his pocketknife. He brings the note close.

JOIN US OUT BACK

The note, Vitri assumes, is an arm of his wife's anger, one without hands, without fingers, just a stump wishing it were whole, able to reach, and grasp, and wring. A desperate reach. A miscalculated reach. A futile attempt to choke answers from a throat with only questions.

Vitri folds the note carefully and shoves it into the breast pocket of his grey thermal shirt. Pulls the house key from his pants pocket and sighs. He anticipates that that's all there will be on the other side of this door: months-old sighs, months-old statements. I alone am not the cause of this world's crumble. I alone am not at fault for the vacancy of our street. I alone cannot jolt it all back to life. Blank stares from their son as the interrogation ensues, a debate of place emerging, the same debate of place that had grown stale long before the blackout.

GET US OUT OF HERE, Vitri thinks the note should've read. It's what it all can be pared down to; it's what this home has been for longer than he'd care to admit.

Inside, light breathes on the living room walls. Photographs are back on the mantle, the plastic crates from which they'd been plucked stacked near the sofa. Candles burn on the end tables and the hardwood floor, saucers beneath to collect wax. More candles are on the dining room table, beside place settings for three, empty ten-ounce glasses and ceramic plates, salad forks and spoons. Two burn on the kitchen counter, near the rack of drying dishes and utensils, candlelight flickering off and on the refrigerator, the cupboard doors.

As much as he prefers how it looks now to how he'd left it that morning—with clothes and debris strewn from front door to back, with soiled dishes all along the counters; the scent of sweat, dead skin and perished food fusing with the scent of the excrement drums—Vitri, just feet inside, cannot stave off his confusion. After locking both of the front door's deadbolts, his steps are slow, tempered. The candlelight plays tricks. His skin appears darker than it actually is, his beard more black than grey. Pronounced are the smudges of soot across his forehead, shaped like commas, as is the exclamation point on the bridge of his thin nose. What the light cannot conceal is the leaping of Vitri's eyes: from floor to table, from dining room to kitchen, from candle to candle, attempting to accurately interpret this crossover, from one world to the next, from the present to the past.

Vitri considers his wife's anger once more, wonders what exactly it has evolved into. Self pity. Resentment. Hatred either masked or illuminated by a scene such as this. It's as far as he allows his mind to stretch before surrendering to his senses. He inhales. Almonds. The candles. Once her favorite. In shutting his eyes, he is thrust back to a scene he revisits often while out and alone, a scene before the boy, before these dark days, a scene he now remembers as the last time these candles were lit: a long, brightly-lit hallway, a half-shut bathroom door, these candles along the sink, his wife's slender figure engulfed in steam, shampoo bubbling on her soaked hair. The Shouting Matches plays from the in-wall dock. Always The Shouting Matches. A distorted F chord. A hoarse hum before diving into the first line. She doesn't sing, though, not once, not ever. But she sways, and her long, heavy hair gently whips from shower wall to shower wall. And over time the sway has expanded for Vitri into a twirl, into a glimpse of breasts and pubic hair, of calves and buttocks flexed with and by the raising of her toes, the ballet lessons she'd taken as a child paying off in the unlikeliest of spaces.

As for his part in the scene, Vitri cannot remember. He cannot remember if he keeps his clothes on and stands in the steam and watches her, if he tosses the store keys on the floor, strips, turns the music up, or down, or leaves it the same, or if he just walks out, unaware that it all can expire—the music, the twirl, the water, the light— unaware that years from now not even his imagination will be able to fit him in.

But Vitri wants that. That scene. He wants this—the tidying, the candles—to represent her half of the apology they've refused to share. If it means they'll make love again, he'll say whatever needs to be said. He'll even cave and tell her what he saw today—the catfish that had washed ashore, the dozens of infant-shaped blankets heaped in the alley behind the ALICO building, the naked man stumbling on the other side of the Brazos, the rings around his neck, the dark scabs from sternum to groin. If she again insists on truth, as brutal as it may be, he'll say it. He'll tell her to pack the truck. He'll tell her that half a tank of gas can get them farther than she thinks. He'll tell her it's finally time to leave Waco, that he can see now that it just won't recover, not even in the boy's lifetime. Because he misses her. The feel of her. Her collarbone beneath his lips, her breasts in his hands. He wants to kiss her, actually kiss her, like he hopes teenagers still do, unconscious of their missteps, teeth clanging periodically, passion far outpacing form.

That, he hopes, is what these candles signal. That, he hopes, is on the other side of the kitchen door. That is in the back yard, waiting for him. They are waiting for him. Her. Their son. All that he is supposed to need. All that he is supposed to want. Vitri takes another deep breath. Opens the door.

Outlining the yard are lit tiki torches, lawnchairs methodically placed between them as if an audience had been expected but was running late. In shadow, two coyotes weighing no more than fifteen pounds apiece stand snout to snout, front paws plunged into a shallow hole, back paws searching higher ground for traction. He watches them. Doesn't step closer. Just watches. Coats gone from the belly up, remaining fur in uneven clumps along the spine, Vitri can see ribs. Can see torsos at work. Gnawing. Tugging.

But it is soundless for Vitri watches, the moments increasingly senseless. His vision blurs. Blackens. His hands and feet tingle. The scent of almonds is replaced but by what he has yet to classify. And then slowly his vision comes back. Sound too. And he watches. Watches as one yanks on a tendon with its teeth, spreads it thin like dough. Listens to the other lap from a blood puddle. Stands like this for two seconds, for four seconds, for ten, for twelve.

He takes the 9mm from his waistband, straightens his arm, and fires. Once, twice, flash-flash, so fast it is difficult to tell if either coyote has been hit, or if the bullets had been close at all. They sprint north together, across the lawn, into another, and into another, until they either fall in defeat or blend into the night.

Vitri brings the pistol back to his waist. He knows nothing can be gained by walking to that hole, but he walks there anyway. He knows a fixed gaze cannot regenerate neck and facial flesh, but he gazes nonetheless. The boy's right eye is a cavern, his cheek a canal, blood and pus smeared across the nose and jaw. The index finger of his wife's left hand has been reduced to bone. Fatty strips of cheek and forearm lay on the dirt like stray puzzle pieces.

But the coyotes did not dig this hole. They did not light the tiki torches. They did not pull the trigger of the .22 pistol in his wife's right hand.

And there it is—the only emotion that Vitri will remember processing in this moment: relief, that the boy's fingers are near his chest, the entry wound inches behind his right ear, as if his mother had whispered for him to stare at the moon.

Vitri pries the pistol from his wife's hand and tosses it on the grass. He retrieves the nearest lawnchair and sets it by the hole. He sits down. Does his best to not stare at them but as he succumbs he feels as if he is at once aging and devolving to a younger self, muscles tightening but skin corkscrewing free, the crow's feet leaving the corners of his eyes but landing elsewhere—a cheek, a calf, somewhere near his throat—never able to depart his convulsing body.

II.

Despite the volume of inanimate objects—bike frames, pots, pans, microwaves, toasters, stray dresser drawers, phone chargers, smashed laptops, the occasional wardrobe on wheels accompanying pillaged suitcases, pants, empty hangers still on bend rods and swaying, objects left by those who fled on sidewalks and public transit platforms, objects for the stubborn and ignorant to clean up or sift through—Calypso St. is clear of what Reyn has been instructed to scan for. Any sign of life is to be indicated by sounding the Jeep's horn—honk for sedans skidding out of alleyways and onto the street, honk for tweakers squatting beneath unhinged shop signs, honk for starved Rottweilers pawing through tipped trashcans, honk for small birds falling like rain, honk for their feathered pools of blood. LOOK FOR LIFE, her mother has re-written on the dashboard with a black permanent marker, the initial characters faded over time, over the months. Beside the phrase: HNK 1 IF FAR, HNK 2 IF CLOSE, KEEP DOORS UNLOCKED.

The small chunks of asphalt chiseled out of the street either by hand or by storm do not require the horn. Nor do the trees, bare, bark paling as if doused in bleach, nor do the shards of glass glinting near the parking meters. Here, on Calypso, Reyn has decided that IF FAR means somewhere near the riverfront, near the grey and blue buildings that once were hotels and whose foundations have since been reduced to floodwalls, should the river rise again. She'll honk twice, then, if threats appear in the dollar store parking lots, or lurk among the shin-high grass of the St. Francis Medical Center campus. And all Reyn can do is hope that her mother will hear it, somewhere in that hospital, whichever floor she is on, whichever staircase, whichever wing or operating room.

Reyn has been inside St. Francis before, at the age of five, for a second opinion on the best approaches for confronting deafness. She remembers her mother as comforting that day, strong, sure, but fragile enough for love. Eyes forward. Straight back. Legs crossed; a bouncing knee. They'd held hands that day, in the elevator, in the waiting room, even while the doctor, a gangly man with a parched scalp, glanced incessantly at Reyn's mother, then leaned back, inhaled, and explained what his examination foretold.

"   deaf mute   different   insurance
        very little   we   do   sorry "

Once home, Reyn's mother, so healthy then, so colorful—a jade sweater with sequins, pinpoint eyeliner, sun-hugged skin—had laid on the couch, on her back, and waved her daughter over. She then grabbed three of Reyn's fingers and placed them on her throat. And she'd hummed there, some slow, jazzy tune, on that blue couch, in that unkempt living room on LaFontaine St.

It's this moment that Reyn wishes she could step back into now. She thinks she'd tidy up the living room, stack the coffee table's stray magazines, straighten the bunched rug, tilt the television so that sunlight no longer interfered with daytime subtitles. She'd then approach her five-year-old self, take her free hand and lead her into the kitchen, sit her down at the lone bistro table and write. Let her know. That she will never hear the kitchen sink drain. That she will never hear her father's heel-driven footsteps, nor the sizzle of his crab cakes in his oil-soaked cast iron skillet. That touching her mother's humming throat is not to be thought of as a game that one day she will win—correctly pinpointing the source of the vibration as a music student would locate notes from plucked harp strings—but only as an exercise of reduction: to smell, to sight, to touch and taste. She'd write that the words and phrases her five-year-old self will soon feel swelling in her gut, that jagged ball working its way into her throat, those beginnings, those embers, will surface only as a written question: WHAT DID IT SOUND LIKE? To which her mother's answer will always be: WHAT?

Reyn hates that she will never know what the Jeep's horn sounds like. She hates that it is this Jeep that connects her and her mother now, not that house on LaFontaine, nor that sofa, nor functioning fingers latched to a functioning throat. She hates that it is her deafness that keeps her here, in the driver's seat, while her mother scrounges for what has replaced everything that she claims has been lost: FOOD, DRINK, MEDS, WORDS.

Day in, day out, these are the items they search for. They are why Reyn spends so many hours in this Jeep, outside of hospitals, clinics and pharmacies. Of course there they'll be upon her mother's return, in her possession, all four, in spades, positioned within the duffel bag just so, atop loose syringes and those rainbow-tinted vials of

Ohapila as if Reyn's mother were still trying to hide the addiction from her daughter. As if she hadn't carelessly stabbed her forearm for the past nine months and plunged the drug into whichever vein she'd struck. As if her eyes wouldn't then widen and immediately yank shut for hours, leaving Reyn, whose lessons in lip reading had come to as abrupt of a halt as everything else, to watch her mother talk. As if those conversations weren't elaborate, as if her head did not roll from side to side, droolng her daughter's name.

"Reyn."

"   Reyn   ."

"   Reyn   ."

It'll happen again tonight, Reyn knows, miles from here, on some rural road's shoulder. She'll point at CAN WE TALK? and her mother will point at NOT NOW and proceed to open her door far enough for the dim interior light to kick on. And she'll go on with it. She'll shiver. Her stained teeth will grind. She'll cringe when the needle breaks skin. And, once her eyes shut, Reyn, as she always does, will tap her mother's shoulder then, her face, as much out of curiosity as it is out of concern, an attempt to understand the drug, the tug it has on the only person in her life. And she'll once again think to herself how sad it is to sit idle and watch someone change so drastically. She'll consider filling a syringe of her own and lying down on the back seat. She'll picture her fingers filled with denim, and digging for more, yanking, struggling to drag her mother out of the Jeep and onto the road. Driving off, leaving her there for someone else to find and claim. Some other junkie she could die with. Staring into the night, she will contemplate exiting this forever—the Jeep, her mother, her home—being free, to choose something better, to choose someone better.

Why she doesn't act upon these thoughts is no mystery to Reyn. It's fear. Fear is why she sits in this passenger seat, scanning Calypso. Fear is what drives Reyn to exit the Jeep each night, and walk to the passenger side, and use her shoulder to shove her mother's legs in far enough to shut the door. Fear not of herself, nor of her mother, but the fear of being left with less than no one. She is a dependent deaf mute. A helpless parasite, she feels, that can only go as far as her host.

Survival, Reyn believes, hinges on that junkie in St. Francis, that junkie that once was a mother, a good mother who, when not leaping from job to job in pursuit of pay and benefits her associates degree from Louisiana Delta rendered elusive, made it a priority to compensate for the one instructor Monroe Public Schools issued to thirty-three disabled children; after her morning shift serving coffee—for a regional chain who, due to a corporate squashing of its failed all-hands-on-deck effort to expand, was forced to evaluate its benefits program, to move the bar from three to six months employment before kicking in—and before her night shift—at a nearby distillery she hoped would eventually have enough room for her on their marketing team, the graphics side, in particular, though she was willing to challenge herself in other arenas—she'd teach Reyn how to read, how to write, how to COMMUNICATE WITH THOSE EITHER UNABLE OR UNWILLING TO SIGN. She'd sit across from Reyn at the bistro table and mouth vowels, consonants, one-syllable words, then two, and three, and four, checking Reyn's accuracy on the legal pads she brought home from the dollar store one Tuesday. She'd spend hours guiding Reyn as she copied onto those same legal pads whole passages from her favorite books, and even more hours going over the reading comprehension questions Reyn would answer when she was at the distillery and leave on her pillow. All of which, as Reyn has thought often, would've been better explained had her mother at some point in her life been an educator. But she hadn't. She wasn't. Zero training. She even admitted time and again to hating school as a child. To hating reading. And yet her mother guided her. She supported her. And, above all else, her mother conversed with her. THEY WON'T TEACH YOU TO MAKE YOUR OWN DECISIONS, her mother wrote more than once, on the rare occasion that Reyn would express frustration or disinterest, THIS WILL. Another time: YOU'RE SO MUCH SMARTER THAN I WAS, THAN I AM. And another: I'M SO PROUD OF YOU. Her mother asked her questions, but not just any question. She asked the right questions. Instead of HOW WAS SCHOOL?, she'd ask, WHAT DID YOU LIKE ABOUT YOUR DAY? If Reyn was frustrated with something, or someone: HOW WOULD YOU LIKE TO HANDLE THE SITUATION? Upon awakening, on a Saturday that she took off from work: HOW DO YOU WANT OUR DAY TO LOOK?

And Reyn wants that woman back, those questions, that concern. She wants to feel important again, important to the only person in her life. Wants her to know that she yearns for the day that they can once more cuddle on the sofa and watch *Little Big Man*, Reyn attentive, her mother nodding off. Wants to tell her how those reading lessons didn't work, that instead of independence they fused within her a need of approval she hoped was satiable. JUST ONCE, Reyn wants to write on the dashboard, JUST ONCE CAN WE TALK? Just once, can they go back? Can they pass one of Reyn's three TIME magazines back and forth, each of them underlining not just their favorite words, but a message—circled syllables of headlines, underlined sentences, a starred slogan? Can they create a code that only the two of them can decipher? Can there be something deeper than this Jeep to bind them once more?

But she is alone. Her mother is gone. Reyn is alone, and she is sweating. She removes the cat-clawed purple and gold LSU sweatshirt her mother snatched last week from a Goodwill whose roof had caved in, and tosses it on the back seat, leaving her in the baggy white v-neck whose off-brown stains still smell of stale coffee. The sweatshirt drops to the Jeep floor, settles atop an unplanned pyramid of empty bottles and cans. Quaker State bottles, Aquafina bottles, bottles of rubbing alcohol, bottles-bottles-bottles, and eye drops, and nasal spray, those that aren't empty marked of its contents either by obvious color, or with OIL, SOAP GAS, WATER, or MED in the same black permanent marker scribbled across the dash and center console. Also strewn across the Jeep's floor, atop a rusted toolkit Reyn's mother has used only to break car windows, are batteries whose value seems to rest solely on the extraction of acid—D, double A, triple A—torn pages of magazines and newspapers to use as toilet paper, rattier clothes than those Reyn currently wears, the occasional dry pen or stubbed pencil, assorted bandannas, one pot, one pan, a sack of brown rice clamped by a hair tie.

Because for reasons of scope she has tilted them at the most extreme of angles, Reyn cranes her neck to view what each Jeep mirror reflects, which is, as it has been for the past hours, nothing but asphalt, the tops of buildings. Intact ruins. She shifts in the seat, tilts her eyes downward momentarily, at her hands, at her blonde-haired forearms, now exposed, oily but bare, save for the smeared ink near the bone, remnants of a gel

18

pen tattoo she gave herself out of boredom. Just her name, in capital letters. She rotates her hand, examines the clear fingernails she liked most when they were turquoise, the hints of dirt packed into her uncallused palms. Reyn hooks her fingers and thumb around her bony right wrist, paying particular attention to the overlap of the two, how her index finger is firmly atop her thumbnail. She has been doing this every day for weeks. A tick forged by nerves, but justified as the only way to chart growth; like marking your height on the kitchen wall. But she also does it because she worries about how emaciated she has become. She can run her fingers over her stomach and count the notches of her abdomen. When the rearview mirrors aren't so severely angled, Reyn can see the knots of her bicep and tricep as she grips the steering wheel. So too can she see just how large her eyes have become.

Reyn releases her wrist only when she sees a side door of St. Francis creep open. She straightens her back, hovers her left hand over the Jeep's horn. The other is over the gearshift, foot at the ready. She has thought of this moment often, of a threat approaching, not intimidated by the horn, not turned away, but instead sparked by whatever noise it does produce, hoisted into a furious pursuit. She has pictured a man of indescribable height and girth dragging her limp mother out of these hospitals by the hair. She's wondered if she could ever leave her mother in a scenario like that, drive off and debate over when it'd be best to return. Has wondered if she has it in her to gun it over the curb, across a sidewalk and lawn, pursuing from the seat of power she does hold, feeling the quick squish of the indescribable man beneath the Jeep.

Please be her, Reyn thinks, *please be her*.

Other than glancing at the ink-covered dashboard and gauges—half a tank of gas remains within the Jeep—she keeps her eyes on St. Francis' door. What appears first, seconds later, is an orange duffel bag. Following, and nudging the stuffed duffel bag along with her shins and calves is Reyn's mother. That black stocking cap. That faded pink jacket. That struggle—in each hands are canvas bags she must've found, misshapen by objects testing their elasticity. She sets them on the grass. Straightens her back, puts her hands on her hips. Squints at the sun. Catches her breath.

Reyn snakes the Jeep through waves of abandoned vehicles—sedans left windowless on the shoulder of the road, pick-ups angled across each lane, a semi tipped entirely, its intricate chassis bled onto by the indigo sky—eventually passing the SHREVEPORT 14 sign and reaching the most open stretch of Highway 20. And there the masked are. Men and women emerge from each treeline as Reyn accelerates, and make their way to the road, topless bodies defined, muscle and tendon swallowing with movement what fat remains. Each face is concealed. Mustard-colored welding masks. Gas masks splattered neon. Trailing are the children. As young as three or four, as old as eleven or twelve, all facsimiles of those they follow: frail bodies, yellow masks, bare feet, even their awkward gait.

For three months now, Reyn has bore witness to this, to them, to this emergence. For three months, she has driven this very stretch of highway, and for three months she has looked at her mother at this very moment, and for three months she has seen the very same reaction, a placidity she has yet to understand. Her mother's shoulders do not tense, nor do her hands. She maintains her slouch. She keeps her eyes forward. Blinks. Again. Again, and again.

An exchange, that's what this is. Trade. Of pills and plastic jugs, of rubbing alcohol and peroxide, of bandages and batteries and beakers, rubber-banded bundles of tongs and forceps, baggies of cotton swabs and iodine, all that currently bulks the duffel and canvas bags on the Jeep's back seat. They do not want the magazines. They do not want the brochures. They don't even want food. Medical supplies are all that the masked desire. In return is gasoline, and oil. In return, freedom is granted—to roam the stretch of highway they have claimed, to search, to resupply, to approach as they are without the onslaught that Reyn pictures happening to unknowing passersby, a blur of yellow swarming tighter and tighter, releasing only when the intruder has been immobilized, corralled to the nearby exit ramps. In return is the only thing Reyn's mother seems to truly desire: Ohapila.

As Reyn understands it, these yellow-masked men and women are its creators. Small bands of them venture into emptied cities each day to scrape paint, rust, and aluminum into buckets that they then lug back and dump into what her mind tells her are enormous cauldrons. What comes next, Reyn isn't certain. She pictures the rubbing alcohol dumped in, the peroxide, the iodine, ingredients of an imprecise process, an unbalanced blend stirred and boiled for hours over an uncontrolled flame far out in the woods, consistency and color a foreign idea, some vials smooth and the color of copper, others choppy and closer to maroon. *Imprecise*, Reyn has thought, because the masked need not care; if there are more like her mother—and there are; she has seen them— there is demand. They need not travel, they need not promote, they need not risk. All will come, and all will pay, and all will return.

For three months, they have returned. Three months, and Reyn still can't help herself from sitting up just that much straighter, from gripping the steering wheel tight with both hands, from feeling as if this somehow won't continue, this trade, how the masked allow their Jeep to approach. *They'll turn soon*, Reyn thinks. *There will soon come a day where the deaf mute and her mother are no longer needed.* Either deemed dispensable, or converted: stripped, fitted with a yellow mask, given a weapon—a claw hammer, a wrench, a hatchet, a screwdriver, a rusted knife—and then a tattoo, of the state, of an eagle, of a gator, of a family tree, a barbed wire or illegible character, any other symbol that stretches across these masked adults, these masked children, across breasts and chests, arms and shins. Escorted to a tree, or ditch, or valley, shown their new home, their new life. It'll happen, Reyn is certain, because progress will deem it so.

Progress: when Reyn's mother first guided her to this outpost, there were ten yellow-masked men and women upon arrival. Now, including the children, there are over eighty.

Progress: just two weeks ago, the masked began construction on their shelter, standing one hundred feet from the highway, between hand-sawn tree trunks. Now, it is the width of a basketball court, and it stands twelve feet tall, a skeleton in place to make it taller, to add a second floor. Now: semi-lit by lanterns placed on surrounding tree stumps, Reyn can see that windows have been found and cut and set aside to wedge into allotted slots.

Progress: Reyn has never seen a pistol in the hands of the masked until this moment, when she pulls the Jeep parallel to the shelter and two backlit silhouettes emerge. The shorter of the two holds the pistol. He is stout despite the living conditions, and wears a marigold welding mask with black specks on its cheeks shaped like teeth. His torso jiggles with each step, belly spilling over his belt loops. The other is tall, torso chiseled, the veins that run from wrist to bicep, from hips to ribs, somehow reflective of the bends and curls of black serpents painted onto the goalie mask tight against his cheeks. As they have done in the past, together they surmount the gentle slope leading to the road. Leaders, Reyn understands.

Progress: the gauntlet converges on the Jeep.

Perhaps, contrary to what they were instructed to do at the start of this relationship, Reyn and her mother are now to exit the Jeep. Maybe Reyn isn't supposed to shut the vehicle off. Maybe they aren't to sit, and wait for the leaders to come to them, negotiating and executing trade through an open window, squishing bags through the frame, contorting both bodies and objects. Maybe Reyn and her mother are no longer welcome here.

But, under her mother's direction, Reyn does not deviate from what has become routine. She rolls down her mother's window, then shuts the engine off. And she stares, first at her mother, who has twisted herself to reach for one of the canvas bags, and next at the tall leader, who has stepped in front of his pear-shaped counterpart and now stands feet from the vehicle. His torso looks to Reyn like what one would find beneath the hood of this very Jeep—power and torque compacted into tubes and parts, into reservoirs and wires. She stares. Even as his eyes find hers, she stares. Even as he tilts his head, as he lowers himself to her level, masked face in the center of the window's frame—she stares.

Reyn's mother hoists the canvas bag over the center console, into Reyn's line of sight. But then she stops. She looks at Reyn—two seconds, three seconds, four—until her message is clear. THAT'S ENOUGH. She then glances down at Reyn's crotch, at the weeks-old bloodstain on the driver's seat. Embarrassed, Reyn bows her head, until the stain is all that she can focus on. To her, it is the only evidence of *her* change, and she is ashamed of it, of her mind's inability to control her body. *It shouldn't have happened here,* she thinks. *It should've happened in a different world, in a bathroom, on that blue couch, or at a*

22

cousin's house, where her mother would be called to pick her up, and they'd drive home, and they'd eat frozen yogurt together, and they'd pass notes back and forth, Reyn's of confusion, her mother's of assurance, of encouragement. *A mother would do that.* A mother would welcome her daughter into womanhood, not ignore requests for tampons or pads because NOT WHAT WE'RE HERE FOR.

Reyn lifts her head when her mother reaches for the second canvas bag. The gauntlet stays put while the leaders step closer. The muscular one grips the windowsill with his right hand, which Reyn can now see has been marked by black ink—JOHN, from left to right, one letter on each knuckle. And she can see his eyes now, through the mask, or some semblance of them, flickers, and then nothing. She watches her mother address him. Watches her jaws stretch. Watches her mouth. Watches JOHN take the canvas bag from her mother and, with planted feet, with so much bend in his torso, pass it to his counterpart. He then points at Reyn. Clearly points, at her.

And back to the stain Reyn's eyes go. The stain. Nowhere else. The stain that she is. The dependent. The parasite. She imagines her mother telling JOHN about her flaws, about her ears, about her dysfunctional tongue. How difficult it has been. How much time she has devoted. How much it still costs her. How she manages. How much better off she'd be if things were different. Ohapila. Back to Ohapila. Back to blackout. Back to comfort.

Reyn the Deaf.

Reyn the Mute.

Reyn the Burden.

A light kicks on. The passenger door is now open. Reyn's mother is stepping outside. Reyn taps the dashboard, fingers not aimed at any particular word, phrase, or command. Her mother turns around, skin like ash under the light, stocking cap already off, raven hair matted. She looks at Reyn not with malice, or concern, but with apology. *For what?* Reyn wonders. She raises her hands to ask. And then her mother's eyes dim into what Reyn interprets as a sad admittance, that where she is going, that what she is about to do, will scar them both.

23

Her mother scribbles her hand in the air until Reyn provides her with a pen from the center console. She leans so her wrist is flat on the dashboard and, when she is done, she caps the pen, and points at what she has written.

SHUT YOUR EYES

Reyn reaches for her mother, but it is too late—she backs her way into JOHN, into the night and, before closing the door, mouths to her daughter: "It. Will. Be. O.K."

And then there is once again darkness, and a panic eased within seconds, as Reyn swivels to see her mother open the rear passenger door of the Jeep. The light comes back on and, after passing the pistol to an osseous man nearby, in climbs the fat man, who, as he slides to the driver's side, sends forward scents of smoke and wood, sweat and paint. Once settled, he frantically nudges his hand beneath his gut and tugs at the button of his pants. Reyn turns around. She does not want to see it, him, his, this. She has seen penises before, but only the bloated cylinders belonging to dead men stripped of their clothes, color the same as the alleyways and sidewalks they rested upon. SHUT YOUR EYES. And, yet, she looks in the rearview mirror as her naked mother, on hands and knees, climbs atop the backseat, puffed eyes like strangled ovals, ribs like foothills to the valley that is her stomach. Only after JOHN follows, only after JOHN shuts the door and strokes himself hard in the darkness, only when he and the fat man are thrusting at opposite ends into her mother does Reyn shut her eyes. The Jeep bounces. Shakes, sways.

And Reyn's mind bends into the afternoons she'd spy on her mother, seated before the open armoire in her bedroom, sun glaring on the makeup kit in her lap. She thinks of the fear she had of being caught, how silly it'd been to be so afraid, but how much more interesting it had made the scene, how intensified it all was—the swiftness of her mother's wrist, the calm, the precision, the faith in the finished product. She thinks of all those times her mother still hoped to impress her father after his long days in that torrid kitchen.

The Jeep shakes. The Jeep sways. Bounces.

Reyn opens her eyes. The masked men and women have advanced on the Jeep. A pair of slender men peer into the driver's side window while four others have gathered on the passenger side, hands shaped like magnifying glasses. Ahead, there are women and children dancing, their weapons piled on the road, arms free to flail. And flail they do, as if their shoulders do nothing to connect one to the other, up-down-around, up-down-around. They stomp. Left-left-right-left-right-right. They jump, they bounce, they slap their thighs as if they are drums. And Reyn feels it. Transmitted to her are synchronized thumps and thuds that soon disband, bleed left, bleed right, left, right, left-right-right-left.

The Jeep sways. The Jeep shakes. Bounces.

Reyn turns around. JOHN's tattooed right hand grips her mother's breast. He no longer thrusts, but half-stands-half-sits, propped by the bent left leg upon the seat. Reyn's mother, seated now, strokes him. Fast, hard, faster, harder. Mirrored on the other side of the backseat is the fat man, masked face tilted back as if searching the Jeep's ceiling for some kind of answer. Small. Stiff. Faster, harder.

The thumps from a man open-hand-slapping the Jeep's quarter panel forces Reyn's eyes to cross into her mother's line of sight. Hair has matted to her damp forehead. She does not blink. When she knows Reyn will not look away, she mouths: "Shut. Your. Eyes."

Which Reyn acknowledges. Which Reyn obeys. She turns around. Closes her eyes. Absorbs the thumps, the thuds, the sound of flesh drums. What follows are visions of yellow masks floating through the night sky, slow, then fast, then slow again, and circling, yellow masks searching for faces, hovering over the Jeep at their own will, crashing into the windshield, jabbing at tires, redirecting the headlights to a faceless crowd of half-naked men and women staring, just staring at Reyn in the driver's seat, one in the distance sculpting a plastic mask with a blow torch, molding it to an infant's cheeks. And the infant grows, evolves rapidly before Reyn's eyes into a woman content atop a lookout tree, happy to stand outside of vehicles like this, and watch events like this, and celebrate moments like this, and stomp to moments like this, and dance.

There is a tap on Reyn's shoulder. She opens her eyes; wakes. The interior light is on. The spectators have vanished. Her mother, clothed now, but looking as if she weighs more than she ever has—shoulders slumped, unable to lift her neck—passes a bowl of stew to her across the seat. Steam rolls into her cheeks. Within the stew are potatoes, carrots, strings of pork. Reyn turns to the back seat. In place of the canvas bags are eight meal-sized cylinders and a bottle of rubbing alcohol. On the seat, atop the emptied duffel bag, are five large jugs of gasoline, a bundle of loaded syringes between, wrapped in twine. Before sitting in the passenger's seat and closing the door, Reyn's mother points to a note she has set on the center console, which Reyn will unfold hours from now and read after the first syringe empties into her mother's arm:

THEY ASKED FOR YOU

They've been here before. West Monroe. Four days ago. And the week before, and the week before that. The same Glenwood Regional swallowed by ivy. Reyn doesn't understand why, if her mother had been at all successful on any of the previous visits, they've come back. She pictures the place stripped of anything useful. Food: gone. Water: gone. Meds: gone. Just a junkie wandering through empty halls, rummaging through empty cupboards, standing in empty ORs.

Yet Reyn writes nothing. She steers where her mother points her, to the ambulance lane. Once parked, she unbuckles her seatbelt, and waits. For something, for anything. In the twelve hours that have passed since she traded her body, Reyn's mother has not been sober—the twine that held the bundle together has been cut, a third of the syringes empty and atop the other junk on the Jeep's floor. Convulsions. Dried blood on her mother's forearm. Dried snot and spit on her mother's cheeks and chin. Everything dry but her jeans, still damp with urine despite Reyn's efforts to soak the mess up with spare shirts, scarves, and gloves.

And now, instead of grabbing the duffel bag and exiting the Jeep, Reyn's mother blankly stares at the glove compartment and twirls her hair. Which leaves Reyn to wonder if she too is questioning why such a sacrifice rested on her shoulders. They could've driven off, sped north, high-tailed it west, and found an exit that, if they could evade the masked men and women, led to a more hopeful life. She could've traded less—left her body out of it, gotten two gallons of gasoline instead of five, six loaded syringes instead of eleven. Reyn could've offered herself instead. She knows that, if her mother had explained what was required of her, she could have done it, handled the both of them, stroked, let them thrust. A fresh young girl is what they wanted. A tight young girl that wears no mask. And at what price? Ten jugs of gasoline? Twenty cans of food? Two-dozen lighters? New tires? One pistol? Permission to drive anywhere they pleased? What of Reyn did her mother's actions protect? How long can and will her actions protect Reyn? How much further along could they be if it had been Reyn in that back seat?

Reyn uncaps a pen and writes on her mother's side of the dashboard: HERE AGAIN? She taps the two words and out of her daze comes her mother, who pulls her stocking cap tight over her head. SHUT IT OFF, her mother writes. SAVE GAS. After Reyn complies, Reyn's mother opens the door, steps out into the morning light, and slumps toward the nearest Glenwood entrance, a gaping hole in a once-automatic glass door. Before stepping through, Reyn's mother turns around. She faces the Jeep, finds Reyn's eyes, and raises her hand. Raises her thumb, her index finger, and her little finger. I LOVE YOU.

The hours crawl. Clouds merge in the sky, then unevenly peel themselves apart, and curl, and thin, evaporating eventually to blue.

Open on Reyn's lap is her favorite issue of TIME. A commemorative issue whose hard cover states, PEACE AT LAST just beneath a photograph of the USS Bataan, the oldest in the fleet, and upon whose topmost deck are men and women with their arms in the air, celebrating the end of the Iranian conflict. In the distance, miles from the aircraft carrier, is the coastline, an elevated city with clay buildings aflame, thick grey streams of smoke unraveling into the sky. 19 SEPTEMBER, 2019. She has read it, several times, from cover to cover—the detailed timeline of the conflict, each and every headline, each and every block quote, each and every word of the personal accounts from soldiers, sailors, and SEAL teams, from the wives and children. None of that, however, is what keeps Reyn returning to this particular issue, the oldest in her collection of three. Words are not what keep her turning its glossy pages.

Near the back of the issue is the smallest of photographs—DADDY, COME HOME, its caption reads, and in it is a camouflaged father, both of his light-haired daughters in his arms, wet cheeks against his clean-shaven neck. Though she has prematurely flipped to this image hundreds of times before, Reyn intentionally prolongs the process now, one page at a time, hoping that doing so will recapture the feeling she had that first time—the smile, the joy, the empathy, the escape. One page. Another. Another. Blindly flipping. Losing interest in blindly flipping. Past an advertisement for headphones, past another promoting the TIME app, past a cartoon with suited men being dropped into a soup bowl of oil by a grey hand three times their size. Another, another, past the American flag, past a flavored vodka ad, two at a time, three, three, three-three-two, until Reyn skips ahead, past the desired photograph, and grabs the back cover, closing the issue altogether.

She reaches beneath the driver's seat and pulls out the others. Calmly places PEACE AT LAST atop the 14 APRIL, 2022 issue, atop WHAT APOCALYPSE?, atop the enormous drill that makes the men working on it look like mice, their heads a third of the VANCE STEEL logos hugging the cylinder. She shoves them back where they belong.

3FAJ172: MICHIGAN
MFV9124: TENNESSEE
084BART: NEW JERSEY
LEV2225: CONNECTICUT
XGZK628: NORTH CAROLINA
B808B92: IDAHO.

The Idaho license plate on the Ford pickup aligns with what Reyn remembers her father's last postcard looking like: mountains, beautiful mountains in a false blue, jagged and with white peaks. He'd written carefully, letters curled where they needed to be, sentences relatively straight across the back of the card. I LOVE YOU, he'd written. I'M SORRY. XOXO.

Reyn remembers the day she walked out to the mailbox and found that postcard. The earliest days of what would become the blackout. TV stations out, yes, cellular towers inoperable, yes, internet connection down, yes, but weeks before the landlines had been uprooted and heaped over asphalt, weeks before buses were hijacked mid-route by men that had just looted local gun stores. Weeks before and, yet, her mother had been voluntarily bed-ridden, quilt to chin, blinds shut and lights left off. She remembers walking that postcard into the house on LaFontaine, sitting on the couch, and digesting every syllable again and again over a span of hours, thinking of how odd it was of her father to declare his love from a distance, and then apologize for the distance, how odd it was to fondly remember his deep slouch, his crooked smile, how odd it was for her to actually believe that her mother would want to go.

She remembers waiting days before attaching a sticky note to the postcard that said, WE CAN GO, and delivering it to her mother, who, hours later, arose, walked down the stairs and proceeded to toss the card into the kitchen sink and drown her husband's last words with the last of the tap water. She remembers the next time her mother came down the stairs, when, as few as six blocks down the street, men and women in grey coveralls and surgeon masks surrounded fled homes, putty knives in hand. She remembers her mother not even bothering to write a note, but immediately packing up the Jeep, ushering Reyn to do the same. She remembers obeying, blindly obeying, climbing into the passenger seat at twelve years old, unaware that her mother's only intention would be to drive around, unaware that on her thirteenth birthday she would be shown how to operate the Jeep, unaware that it would be the place that she'd become a woman. Unaware that, in the beginning, she would look at the license plates of abandoned vehicles and hope that whomever its owner was had somehow made it safely home amidst the chaos, with their high-powered flashlights, with quarter-sized candles in their palms. Unaware that something incomprehensible within her would turn, that she would eventually look at these license plates and think only of herself. Where they could be right now. How far out of Monroe they could've gotten.

A lone pigeon bobs awkwardly on the sidewalk, pecking at debris as the breeze tumbles it by. The way it moves hints at injury, the majority of its weight on one narrow leg. Its breast is closer to bone. When the sun hits it just right, there is a pea green shimmer on the remaining feathers, a dark red gloss to its left eye. The pigeon stops and thrashes its head in a series of diagonals. Chaos rooted in scheme. Seconds later, off the pigeon goes, back on track, bobbing down the sidewalk, persistent in its search.

Reyn looks at the knuckles on her left hand. REYN, they read, one large, deeply shaded letter on all but the thumb. She then stares at the hole in the glass door, where her mother entered the hospital. Not much else of the building's interior can be seen from the driver's seat; darkness, mostly, slivers of light illuminating ten feet inward, making clear only the tile floor.

Any minute now, Reyn thinks. *Any minute now*, her mother will walk through that hole, goods in tow. So many things, Reyn hopes, things they've proven they don't need, but things that'll make them each smile, that'll make them each forget, forget it all, if even for a moment. Plastic containers of peanut butter, jelly and honey anchoring the bottom of a bag her mother lifted, bruised but edible apples and kiwis between. Another bag in the other hand, this one full of toilet paper and tampons, bars of soap and bundles of books—actual books—shampoo and chewing gum. *Any minute now*, she thinks, *any minute now, any minute now.*

LOOK 4 LIFE
HNK 1 IF FAR
HNK 2 IF CLOSE
KEEP DOORS UNLOCKED

THEY ASKED FOR YOU

KEEP DOORS UNLOCKED
HNK 2 IF CLOSE
HNK 1 IF FAR
LOOK 4 LIFE

Reyn steps through that hole in the Glenwood Regional door. Once past what had been visible from the Jeep—that initial burst of light—Reyn sees that each of the forking hallways before her are strewn with bodies. Still bodies, child bodies, adult

30

bodies, rotting bodies, black bodies, white bodies, naked bodies, bodies cut open, bodies with surfacing bones, bodies whose legs and backs and faces are pressed to the walls, a small path between bodies to walk upon, an arm here and there to step over.

The smell alone causes Reyn to vomit. Scavengers have been dragging these bodies, stacking them, manipulating them to ensure mobility. Syringes populate the path, a few sticking out of forearms like diving boards over taut pools of grey. Once the vomiting is over, once her body allows her brain to resume its function, Reyn can't help but wonder if each and every place that her mother enters is like this, an incinerator awaiting heat. If so, she cannot fathom how her mother has done it, how she has gone so long without saying so, and has instead absorbed the assault on her senses and re-entered the Jeep looking the same as when she'd exited.

Reyn begins down the left hallway, which, of the two, holds more light. Head up, eyes up, averted from the bodies, she passes examination room after examination room, each either with its door partially open, or with shotgun holes as doorknobs. Within these rooms, Reyn can see, are anatomical diagrams, clear jars of tongue depressors and cotton balls. And more bodies. Far fewer than the hallway but three or four to each, some scattered, some stacked unnaturally near, or against, the respective door.

At the end of the hallway, adjacent to a pair of elevators, is a doorway cleared of bodies, but also void of its floor directory, reduced to a rectangle of dry glue. Reyn opens the door. Dim light from the hallway seeps into the dark room, a breath long enough to see the staircase, wide enough to see that ten feet from the bottom step crouches a naked man with eggshell skin and scraggly hair the color of rust. Reyn looks to the floor. Diarrhea splatters on the tile, onto the blue and pink cloths over his feet. The man twists at the torso, rotates his gaunt face toward Reyn. Somewhere in that beard are his lips, somewhere he is saying something to her. But Reyn, only seeing the red blade of the scalpel in his right hand, lets go of the door. She sprints up the stairs, sprints-sprints-sprints, the room growing darker and darker as she goes, as she tackles another flight, her hand dragging across the wall, hoping to find a door handle. Once she does, she quickly flings the door inward and steps into a hallway just as dark, save for a haze of daylight at its apparent end, one hundred feet away. There is no time. She steps toward that light, telling herself that the bearded man will not follow, that, if he does, he will not find her, that he will not grab her with jagged fingernails, that he will not shove her face onto the tile and thrust his dick into her. He will not rape her, and he will not kill her because she will not let him.

As she'd done on the stairwell, Reyn extends her arm to the wall and feels her way forward, first at a walk, but then, as she becomes acclimated, stalking faster and faster and faster, fingers grazing dried splotches of something she refuses to inspect. Every few steps, she turns around, expecting that bearded man, some shape to break from the dark. Faster, faster, almost to a jog now, and faster, and faster, until she no longer can step, but only slide. She falls to the floor. Liquid splashes onto her neck, onto her sweatshirt. Smells of vinegar. She quickly removes her right foot from the bedpan but, in so much of a hurry, Reyn trips once more before sprinting to the hallway's end, arms locked to brace her impact with the wall.

The light comes from east-facing windows along another hallway. On the windows, on the bits of wall between, are red handprints, red streaks to the bottom. To Reyn's immediate right is another staircase, this one's floor directory intact. There are four floors altogether. *There is no reason to go up*, Reyn thinks, *no reason at all*. Her mother has left by now. *She is outside*, at the Jeep, *locked out and waiting. Make your way down. Hurry*. Yet, in nearing the windows, Reyn can see that the red handprints are still slick. She looks at the tile floor. More red. More streaks. More handprints.

And so Reyn follows the trail down the hallway. It grows thicker as she approaches an open door. She looks up. To the left, behind an entire wall of glass, are newborns still bundled in their blankets, color-coded by gender, some faces nearer to skeletons than others but most like mush, soft flesh caving in on itself. Untouched, in rows, elevated as something sacred.

The trail of blood extends further into the room, past the first row of babies, past the second, and proceeds into a curve, which Reyn follows. There, at the end of it, is her mother, curled not unlike an infant, and bloody. All over her hands and wrists. Smeared across her face. Reyn does not hurry to her, nor does she drop to her knees. But she approaches. Once there, she crouches. She examines her mother. Sees the puncture in her throat; thinks of the scalpel. Thinks of the bearded man. Taps her mother's shoulder. Places the back of her hand against her cheek. Warmth leaving her skin. Eyes, chest: motionless. Reyn pulls her hand back but remains crouched. Looks at her mother. Looks elsewhere, at the floor, at the blood, at the babies, at her feet. At the glass enclosing all of this, wondering when the bearded man will come, wondering how long she has with her mother before she's forced to sprint.

III.

Vitri unlatches the charcoal grey carrying case his 9mm pistol came in. He takes the pistol from its fitted slot in the foam and sets it on the stand separating him from range and target. Nearby is the 500-count box of ammunition he purchased earlier that morning from the Cabela's near Cottonwood Creek, its flip-top open, precisely stacked rounds reminding Vitri of the wagonfuls of straw he often sees between cities, while en route to designers, to neo-hipsters at small-town markets. Before grabbing the empty clip from the carrying case and subsequently inserting the rounds, Vitri backs into the partition separating him and the slender man that wipes his mustache after a series of revolver draws. He looks at his wife, standing adjacent, honey-colored hair pulled back, arms folded, safety-glassed eyes drifting from shooter to shooter, muffed ears no match for the shotgun blast of the husky woman at the end, in the white A&M sweatshirt, stock firmly against her shoulder. Vitri grabs a round from the top of the stack and shoves it into the clip.

"You okay?" Vitri asks, when the shooting slows. His hair is short, cropped, the fade from sides to scalp filling in. Three days of stubble have blackened his husky cheeks, his chin and neck.

Eyes on the smoke above the A&M woman, Vitri's wife nods. "Yeah," she says. "Yeah, I'm great, Vitri. How are you doing? You look tough holding that thing. Do you feel tough? Does holding that thing make you feel tough?"

"Maybe it does," Vitri says, as calmly as he can, insistent on not letting her see how much this irritates him, the way she talks down, the way she shits on everything that excites him. But he says something true. Something he accepted the week before, when he fired off thirty-six rounds behind Mel's Handguns & Accessories, walked over to Gavin, the overseeing sales associate, took off the same safety glasses he wears now, and gave him a look that said, *This is the one*. Because it *does* make him feel tough. It *does* make him feel strong. It makes him feel something she never could: a scream without the scream, a contained freedom slow-released through this trigger finger

"That doesn't explain why I'm here," Vitri's wife says. The slender man, finished with his session, walks past, revolver back in its hip holster, and nods. Vitri's wife nods back.

Vitri steps closer to her. "I want you to know how to use it. I want you to be able to protect yourself."

She finally faces Vitri. "From who? You?"

"What does that mean?" Vitri asks. But he knows. He has watched her slowly pull her jeans over the bruises along her hips, the welts on her backside. Her bottom lip is still swollen from the thrust that drove her face into the dresser. He lowers his voice: "You used to tell me to do shit like that to you all the time."

Vitri's wife stares downrange, at black targets with white rings, dime-sized holes sprayed from top to bottom, side to side. "Maybe I never did it for me." She lifts her safety glasses enough to rub the inside corner of her left eye. "Maybe I never wanted it, maybe I never—"

"Well," Vitri interrupts, "I want this. I like this." He raises an open hand and fans it as if encompassing the width of the room. "And I hope you like this too." He tries to give her the most understanding look that he can, one that says, despite his tone, he knows how distant they've become, that this tone, this conversation, is a façade, that it's only this way because his tongue won't work when he tries to tell her that he wants what they once had. "Just come over here, please."

Vitri's wife goes, eventually. After watching Vitri fire an entire clip at the target, she walks to him. She watches him load the pistol for her. Bites her lip as he arranges her sore hips into whichever angle he feels is best. Listens when he tells her to relax, and breathe.

Both pistols lie side by side on the bench seat of the S10, barrels pointed in opposite directions. The red backpack on the floor tips over when entering a sharp curve. Keys clang as the truck accelerates.

Vitri can't help but squint. He has not slept. He has not eaten. His eyes have been rubbed pink. Sweat has dampened the burgundy scarf he keeps over his mouth and nose. When the sun slinks behind one of two clouds, Vitri's eyes ease into an unblinking stare, forward, and with determination.

He'll run out of gas before he hits Tyler. He knows he will. He knows he will be stranded, and that he will walk through this flatland. He'll walk, alone, and he'll try to survive. He'll try, and try, and if he doesn't, so be it. So be it.

For the sixth time since leaving Waco, Vitri reaches into the breast pocket of his grey thermal shirt and pulls out a slip of paper. A note. A different note. Vitri unfolds, glances down.

872 E JUNIPER GROVE
TALLAHASSEE, FLORIDA

"Eight-seven-two, east Juniper Grove," Vitri says, his voice hoarse, a terra cotta soldier just woken, and with orders, arms and legs cracking to life, debris tumbling. "Eight-seven-two, east Juniper Grove, eight-seven-two, east Juniper Grove."

The sun has launched its pink and orange tendrils into the night. A few of the kitchen candles still burn, the rest snuffed out by the breeze stirring through the open back door. Vitri approaches, his breathing labored, and swivels through the doorframe. The boy is in his arms, cradled, but unable to fit like he once was, heavy head angled at the floor, chin pointed at the ceiling, dangling arms and legs bent like manipulated wire. Without pause, a scarf-free Vitri walks to the staircase, turns his body sideways and carries the boy up the carpeted stairs, head first, past the ascending picture frames on the wall—the first of Vitri and his wife's wedding day, tux and gown clean but each of them with cake smears along their cheeks, gobs of frosting on their fingers. The second: Vitri and his wife on the bow of the *American Queen*, backs against the railing, overcast sky above, a calm river below. The last is of the boy and his entrance into this world, skin blotched red, wisps of damp hair across his scalp, a light blue blanket around his torso.

Once atop the stairs, Vitri, still turned sideways, carries the boy past his room, past the bathroom, and into the master bedroom, path not guided as much by light as it is by memory, by repetition. No candles burn on this second level. Only darkness, save for the slivers of sunlight jutting through the slim cracks of poorly boarded windows. It's enough to see that the floor has been cleared of clothes and shoes, of coat hangers and nails, all other things that had been thrown and ignored. It's enough to see that the bed has been made—quilt pulled tight, all pillows where they once were intended. It's enough to see the pistol case at the foot end of the bed, orange in color, and open.

Vitri eases the boy to the mattress. He rolls him onto his back. Carefully angles his arms; places one hand over the other. Then, he swiftly reaches for the pistol case, shuts its top and strides through the bedroom, past the bathroom, down the stairs, past it all, opening it once back in the kitchen.

A bore brush. Stray rounds. Gun oil. A patch holder, its patches. Cotton swabs and a cleaning rod. The only thing missing from the case is the pistol; the only thing out of place is a note, written on the back of a convenience store receipt and taped to the foam itself. Vitri peels the note off and holds it over candlelight.

IN CASE THINGS GET WORSE FOR YOU TWO.
-CARMEN

Carmen. His wife's cousin. Carmen, the ginger-haired County Clerk that loves dogs but hates strays. Carmen, the conspiracy theorist with a government job, living in a bungalow on wheels that she had begged an ex-boyfriend to buy. Carmen, who would refuse to apply sunscreen to her sallow skin but who would lie under the sun for hours on end, top off, chest down, her back folding in on itself by day's end. Carmen, who defiantly claimed not to drink but who would swig the better half of someone else's bottle of wine. Carmen, the activist of nothing important. Carmen: Vitri's wife's only confidante. Chapter-length emails evolving into text messages while stalking department store aisles for Christmas toys. Texts to phone conversations, the bathroom door shut for the duration of an afternoon, no steam to speak of.

###

"Tell me something," Carmen says. It is a summer evening. The kitchen window is open. Merlot has intensified Carmen's already-liberated tongue. She adjusts the shoulder strap of her thrift-store sundress. "I'm only asking because I love you," she adds, "but are you happy here?"

She sits at the dining room table but speaks at a volume that Vitri, who is outside and tending the grill with an oversized metal spatula, can hear her, even over his wife's opening and closing of cupboard doors. He flips the hamburger patties and rotates Carmen's veggie kabob, wishing the cumulative sizzle were louder, deafening even. He pictures Carmen on mute, sitting on the sofa, mouth moving, hands as accents, but with no result. Not a thing. Messages unsent. Lost, reverted back to their source. He could handle that Carmen. Laughs at the image of that Carmen. Yet he says nothing. Closes nothing, flips nothing. Does nothing but check his cell phone for the time—7:33. When he looks through the kitchen window, he sees his wife walking toward Carmen, wine bottle in hand.

"Here as in Waco?" Vitri's wife asks. She tops off Carmen's glass, pours her own, then sits at the table.

"Be serious," Carmen says. "We both know you've wanted out of Waco for a long time. What I mean is here, as in your life. Are you happy with it?"

One day. That's all Vitri needs to do: stay strong for one day. Stay strong until she attends whatever-the-hell conference that has brought her here from Tallahassee, until she goes to sleep, until she shoves the top end of that kabob in her mouth.

Vitir's wife swirls her wine glass. Sips. "Why do you ask?"

"You remember when we used to go to PopPop's for Thanksgiving? I'd bring my boyfriends, you'd bring yours, and at night, after the old fucks passed out—as chilly as it was, as stuffed as we were—we'd all pocket the leftover booze and sneak off to the bluff? We'd have the bottles empty by the time we got there? You remember that?"

"I do."

Vitri looks through the window again. Wishes it didn't bother him that his wife is smiling. Wishes he could stop himself from straining to hear what he hopes is exclusively a recollection of PopPop—a man he has only seen in a casket, grey hand over grey hand—and not Jeremy, not Chris, not some man-child that left her long before meeting him, when she was twenty-seven and he thirty-one. He moves a mound

39

of charring meat to a cooler corner; watches the coals ignite the excess. *You're too old*, he tells himself, *for liquor bottles atop bluffs. Too old to be jealous over a time that didn't belong to him.*

"I think that was the happiest you I've ever seen." Carmen waits for a response, a rebuttal, something. "Look, it isn't like I'm around you twenty-four-seven, but I'm not an idiot. You're paler than I am. That new diet has you looking like a skeleton. Your eyes—"

"Jesus Christ, Carmen," Vitri's wife says. She glances at she and Vitri's son, on the suede recliner in the living room, television glow on his face, floor fan pointed at his legs. "Give a warning the next time you're going to attack me."

"I'm not attacking you; I'm trying to help."

"Calling someone a skeleton doesn't seem like help."

"Because it's honest?" Carmen asks. "You want me to tell you that you look radiant? That I like the way your straps keep slipping off of your shoulders? Is that what you want to hear? Is that what Vitri tells you?"

"Don't bring Vitri into this, Carmen."

Carmen shakes her head. "It is, isn't it? He probably tells you every other day how pretty you are, how comfortable your sunken eyes make him."

Vitri can't help but feel pity in this brief moment of silence, for Carmen, for the malice in her tone, for her disapproval of him. He is beyond anger with her. Anger was when she vomited on her plate after giving her maid of honor speech at their wedding. Anger was the first time she came back to Waco, when she knocked on their bedroom door at 3:00am and asked if Vitri would sleep on the couch.

"Who wouldn't want to be complimented?" Vitri's wife says.

"That doesn't mean that you're happy. Look," Carmen says, "that girl back at PopPop's, that girl up on that bluff, she didn't need a compliment to feel good about herself, about the world. That girl spoke eloquently, and she spoke often—to me, to each of those drunken boys—about the pursuit of an extraordinary life. 'I'm going to live in Dublin,' that girl said. 'And Lisbon, and Brussels. I'm going to design evening gowns for the world's royalty, I'm going to climb over the Great Wall, I'm going to run with the bulls—"

40

Vitri's wife laughs with Carmen. "I never said that," she says.

"Whatever," Carmen says, "Let's say you didn't. Still, have you done anything a younger you intended to do?"

Silence.

"When was the last time you left Texas?" Carmen asks.

Vitri flips. Vitri rotates. He can't even answer that question. Years, he knows.

Carmen persists: "Do you think that's a good thing? Does that represent a high quality of life to you?" She lowers her voice, looks at the boy, then back at her cousin. "What about him?"

"Let's keep this about me, okay," Vitri's wife says.

Carmen sighs. Gulps wine. Wipes her mouth with her wrist. "I grew up here, too. I know how little opportunity there is. And I look around now, not just at you, but at everyone here, and, more than ever, I just can't understand how these people can so readily accept mediocrity, and, more importantly, how these people can treat their children like chicken breasts and inject them so deeply with that desire for mediocrity. Because why? For flavor, to feel better about their own life, that they, quote-unquote, didn't do such a bad job?"

Vitri sighs. He briefly picks at an ingrown hair on his stubbled chin. *Tell her she's wrong,* he thinks. *Go on, tell her. Tell her that Tallahassee is no exotic destination; tell her that Waco is no dumping ground. That he isn't either, that she isn't, that none of them are, that Carmen's words aren't welcome here. Tell her that a one-week trip to Madagascar doesn't make her a world traveler; only a single, childless woman riddled with false empowerment. Tell her that she's a hypocrite. Shout it all. Who cares if the boy hears? Who cares if it scares him into turning the TV off and facing this heat with his father? Do it.*

"Carmen, I—"

"I want what's best for you," Carmen interrupts, "and I want what's best for him. If that includes Vitri, if that includes Waco, then fine. Tell me and I'll shut up."

"You'll just stop? On a dime, just stop?"

"If you can sit there, look me in the eye, and tell me that you aren't spending your days wondering if Vitri is manipulating you into accepting an existence you never intended, then, yeah, I'll shut the fuck up."

Do it. Say it. Shout.

Vitri's wife laughs. The laugh fades. "And what if it doesn't?"

"Doesn't what?"

"Doesn't include Waco," Vitri's wife says. "Doesn't include Vitri."

At that, Vitri grabs the serving dish from the side table of his gas grill, into which he sets all of the hamburger patties. He shuts the grill off and, before going inside, before turning at all, lifts the largest patty he'd made and squeezes. Hamburger blood drizzles over Carmen's kabob skewer. Over the blackened zucchini, over chunks of onion, over the baby carrots.

When he does walk through that back door, he is greeted by both Carmen and his wife. "It smells so good," they say in heightened tones, and, "I'm starving," to which Vitri says nothing. He tosses the serving dish on the counter, grabs his keys and walks toward the front door, stopping only when his wife reaches for his hand.

"I thought we were all going to eat together," she says.

"I can't stomach that," Vitri says.

"Oh, come on, Vitri," Carmen says. "Sit down, have a glass of wine with us."

"Fuck off, Carmen," Vitri says, then continues toward the front door. He stops near the living room and stares at his son. "Hey," Vitri says and, without the boy's attention, continues, "let's leave these cunts alone to talk about wasted lives."

"What?" the boy says.

And then Vitri is gone, out of the house, down the steps, down the sidewalk and to his truck, too upset, too focused on escape to look at Carmen's sedan, at the orange case peeking from beneath the passenger seat.

Vitri swerves the S10 to the right of a stray fender, then powers the truck up a hill partially shaded by grey-barked cottonwoods, a relief for his eyes that won't last for more than a mile. East, he thinks. To Tallahassee, Florida. Eight-seven-two, East Juniper Grove. He sighs. The scarf over his mouth has dampened with sweat and saliva. He places the note back into his breast pocket. *Because you do things when you're angry. You go places.* He grips the steering wheel tighter. Glances at his reflection in the rearview mirror. *You're going to Tallahassee, Florida and you're going to do whatever it takes to get there.*

Vitri lies in the middle of his bed, between his dead wife and dead son. He has shut their eyes but, like them, his hands are over his bellybutton, calm, folded, fingers too numb to fight or search for their counterpart. Slinked around his neck is the burgundy scarf. And atop his chest is his 9mm pistol. Twice now he has shoved the barrel into his mouth and twice now he has pulled it out. Thoughts continue to flood. Ooze out of his earholes, out of his nose and throat. The first time he put the barrel in his mouth, he was transported back to the store, to that afternoon when another man's pistol was aimed at his face. He remembered the smell of the man long after that afternoon, rather than the look of him, the stale sewage on his coverall sleeves, the hash browns on his breath, the desperation of a man with nothing.

The second time took him to this very room. Bed gone, dresser gone, TV gone, periwinkle curtains and oak closet door, all gone. Empty. For sale. His wife's hand in his. A shirt and tie causing him to stand straighter, to puff his chest. The taste of a late lunch still on his lips. Though it was nearly two years before his time, he pictures the boy there, too, sprinting up and down the stairs in his t-ball uniform and cleats, no bat in his hand, not even a glove. Nothing. But he stops. He looks at his mother and father. No smile. No frown. A gaze that just says, "What? Do something."

An audience. That's what has stopped Vitri from going through with it, from closing his eyes, nestling the barrel against his palate, and squeezing the trigger. Fear, real fear. One that a man cannot rid himself of, present since birth and evolving as its host does, flexing, twisting, tweaking itself over time. Over knee scrapes and heart breaks. Over lost jobs and uncertainties.

As dead as they are, Vitri wants to believe that they are sleeping, that his son will wake first, and then his wife, and that this, this moment—when they nearly bore witness to his admittance of failure—will be forgotten, placed in the wrong drawer, tucked neatly with the useless.

And so he rises. He looks once at his son, and once at his wife. Then, pistol in hand, he scoots himself off of the bed and walks down the stairs. He goes directly to the cupboard just left of the dark and silent refrigerator, on whose door, held in place by an *American Queen* magnet, still hangs a strip of white paper, 872 E JUNIPER GROVE printed across the center, CARMEN signed beneath TALLHASSEE, FLORIDA. But that doesn't matter now. What does is that, without hesitation, Vitri removes the gold band from his left ring finger and sets it on the bottom of that open drawer. What does matter is that he exchanges it for a small bottle of lighter fluid, a third of the way full, its nozzle layered in dust. Vitri shoves the pistol in his waistband and uses his free hand to lift one of two candles from the dining room table that, though its wick is nearly drowned in hot wax, has yet to burn out. He carries the candle to the staircase and carefully squats to the second step. Squirts lighter fluid on the edge. Tilts the candle. The flame ignites, gnaws the carpet. Smoke straws roll. Quiver. Dissipate. He rotates the candle. More smoke. And, though it struggles to spread, a flame eventually holds. Vitri stands. Watches. Aims the plastic bottle and squeezes like hell, arcing the stream up, up-up-up.

Vitri runs out of gas miles south of Tyler. Clouds have leaked into blue. The sun is high, searing. He needs to find shade, none of which appears to be north. No, as far as he can see, north is a continuation of this valley, a sweltering flat road flanked by fields of corn and hay that are now shriveled gray and dusty, tractor-hauled boulders between. A few hundred yards to the east are parallel treelines, trees themselves like stick figures of a child's drawing, primed to sprout sets of spindly legs and stride over this valley, over Vitri, over the truck, though their leafless branches would provide only a fraction of the shade he seeks.

Vitri gets out of the truck. Before walking to the passenger door, he unties the scarf. In the sun his coal black hair is tinted silver, warm to the touch. He proceeds to tie the scarf in a different fashion while walking, the main point of pressure being his forehead. He knots it behind his head and lets what remains flap down over the back of his neck. For the most part, it works, though an inch or two of flesh is still exposed, sure to be pink within an hour.

Vitri grabs the backpack from the truck's floor and unzips its largest pocket. He places the .22 pistol inside the backpack, its barrel hoisted by the two bundles of socks at the bottom. Just inches to the right, atop a Ziploc bag of almond-scented candles, and slinked around a teepee of three plastic water bottles, is a pair of unfolded boxer briefs. One metal fork is astray, as is one metal spoon, and a toothbrush with warped bristles he'd found in the cupboard beneath the kitchen sink. A bar of soap is wedged between two aluminum cans of tomato soup, flanked by granola bars in metallic green wrappers, all past their expiration date. As it has been doing since exiting Waco, Vitri's stomach groans, tightens. It has been over twenty-four hours since his last bite, since he used his pocketknife to carve out the edible part of an apple he found near the Brazos. He should eat. He needs to eat.

Yet all he does is zip the backpack shut, and shove the 9mm into his waistband. He pats his front pockets. The pocketknife is there. The moist towelettes, securely in their wrappers. He pats his breast pocket, which is inflated by the folded note. Then, after slinging the backpack over his shoulders, Vitri shuts the S10 door for the last time, and starts east on foot, truck keys dangling from the ignition.

Vitri rests beneath a young hickory tree on the shoulder of the road whose bare limbs provide wedges of shade. His makeshift turban is heavy with sweat. He digs into his backpack for a bottle of water and, without so much as a thought about conservation, takes one large gulp, and another, until there are only droplets clinging to the sides of the plastic.

Vitri doesn't bother shoving the empty bottle back into his backpack, but tosses it toward the broken fence separating a hay field from the road. Outside of his own movements, and the distant honking of a lone goose, he has yet to hear a thing. Not an engine, not an ax heaving through a block of wood, not a voice, nothing. Here, though, it somehow smells more like spring, like, somewhere in those fields, in those overgrown oceans of yellow and grey, some sort of flower is blooming. Lilacs. Tulips. Hydrangeas. Something whose wind-carried scent is potent enough to negate the smell of smoke that still clings to his clothes and beard.

It isn't at all what he'd imagined he'd encounter. He'd envisioned fields burnt black, downed power lines sprawling across the roads, twisting themselves around splintered, centuries-old trees. He'd envisioned gutted vehicles, limbless wanderers with teeth that had been filed to blood-stained points, somehow still polite enough to ask for something before taking, but only once. Waco, he'd convinced himself, had been a safe haven, a place one shouldn't venture too far from, a place one would regret leaving as they entered what in his mind had become a wasteland.

Not yet being proved right is what terrifies Vitri most.

Three miles. Three miles, and no shelter, no homes whatsoever, just abandoned tractors he'd taken to be traps. Three miles, and the balls of his feet already are on fire, flat arches unsupported in his boots. The pain surges to his *old* shins, seems to skip his *old* thighs altogether and expands in his *old* lower back, *old* hip to *old* hip.

Fifty yards from the road is a pen of dirt and shit housing dead cattle that look like shells of themselves, their heads the same size as they'd always been but their frames shrunken, stomachs deflated. Eight in all are dead, at different stages of decay. Nearest to the road is the bull, skull at an angle, one horn plugged into the dirt.

Winded from the incline, Vitri reties the damp scarf around his mouth and nose, picturing their owner diligently feeding them early each morning, thinning their portions as things worsened, refusing to give in altogether. He pictures the farmer unable to admit to himself that what he had worked so hard for had been lost, that anything had to be saved.

Behind the pen is a small storage barn. Ten-by-ten at best, its doors open, its interior empty save for flakes of hay that wind has yet to gust out. Vitri intends to walk past the pen, to go inside that shelter, to search for anything that may have been left, to sit down, to rest, if only for half an hour. But he opts to catch his breath while staring at the ruins.

###

Vitri lies in the blood-stained hole his wife dug, a static morning sky before him. A pale blue abyss. Not one cloud. He listens to the flames swallow the top half of his house. Paint sizzling. Wood popping, nails snapping free in the orange swell. It will become unrecognizable, remnants of the past strewn on asphalt, on grass, in this very hole, something for wanderers to pluck, examine, and pocket, not once considering what the completed puzzle could've looked like, the sacrifice to have it so. It is to cave on itself, structure lost, misplaced, reduced to particles hysterically searching for purpose.

Smoke floats high over Vitri, first in strands, and then in braids. He tries to breathe it in, to fill his lungs with what fills the sky. He closes his eyes. He readies the 9mm. Opens his mouth. Edges the barrel past his front teeth. Takes a deep breath—

—and it is night, and he is upright, wearing exactly what he wears now—tan boots and all, burgundy scarf secure around his nose and mouth—and he is on a beach, a beach that, if the palm trees whose tops are aflame speak truths, stretches for miles. But there is no sound. Flaming leaves fall to the damp sand, but the branches do not crackle. Black waves in high tide eddy ashore, but there is no crash, no swirl back, rhythm only seen, not heard.

He steps toward the nearest flaming palm, thirty feet away. He steps again, and again, and again, its warmth overwhelming him to the point of altering his path, however slightly, boot prints arcing to the right of the tree.

Forward. Forward. Forward.

Hundreds of feet down the coast emerges from the black waves a woman, skin pale, luminous in the night. A journeying beacon that, when he sees her, brings Vitri to a stop. He turns. Strains his eyes. Watches her spot him. He considers running, turning the other way and sprinting, spooked enough to not look back, at her, at the sand his boots fling behind him. Yet there he stays. He stays, and she advances, her steps long but calculated, driven by toes instead of heel, heron-like. Moments pass, but she does not increase her pace. Long, careful, segments of her slender body rendered visible by the glow of the palm tree nearest her. Calves he's never seen. A groin he's never seen. Narrow hips he's never seen, a slim torso and small breasts. There seems to be a smile on her face. A genuine smile. Nothing crooked, nothing concealed. But she tilts her head; Carmen wrings out her wet red hair and—

—eyes, open. Smoke cloud. Barrel out, sit-up-stand. Vitri wobbles across his backyard, achieving clarity once he is a dozen feet from the door. He looks around. At the hole. At where the grill once stood year-round.

She ruined you.

Before he enters his burning house, Vitri places the pistol in his waistband. He uses both hands to lift the scarf from neck to mouth.

###

Vitri hears it before he sees it. South of the road one hundred yards or so, he spots the white Suburban whose engine had moments ago idled so brutally. At its sight, Vitri, still with that damp scarf over his mouth and nose, immediately takes cover in the roadside weeds. Crouched there, he pulls the 9mm from his waistband and proceeds to watch the vehicle. Across the dirt road it's parked upon stands a one-story building made of untreated wood that does have a sign, but whose size renders it illegible from this range.

Five minutes pass. Still crouched, Vitri thinks that he should just go, just keep going on foot, east, hurry past that dirt road. *Because that Suburban isn't yours.* It belongs to someone else, perhaps some gruff man with a scoped rifle, a litter of children at home to whom he'll feed anything. In the still-idling vehicle could be dead animals, dead humans, bodies criss-crossed like mulch bags. *The gas tank is probably nearing empty. There is probably less than a quart of oil remaining. It isn't worth it.*

Vitri advances through the field toward the white Suburban. He can see now that its windows are open and, unless they are lying down, no human heads are inside. This gruff man—if it is a gruff man at all—has to still be within what Vitri can now read as haRd WeaR. The sign's vibrancy says that it was painted recently, above the door, in some cousin of mint green. Vitri could believe it. He could imagine it as a center for commerce, an operating establishment that exchanges screws and nails, hammers and rasps for skulls and kidneys, for sex or slaughter, whatever has become currency. A place to gain information. A place to find help. But he doesn't, and there is no way he will. *Trap*, he is convinced. *It is a trap.* Going inside haRd WeaR means pain, means death, one he'd never ask for.

Fifteen yards from the suburban, Vitri, increasing his pace, emerges from his crouch. Faster, faster yet, until he is within arm's length of the Suburban. Despite how rusty it is, how mud-splotched, its exterior smells of vanilla. He eases the grip on his pistol and peers through the Suburban's windows. No bodies, no tools, no wood. A large, unlabeled aluminum can is on the floor, a plastic spoon next to it. Hanging from the rearview mirror is a Black Ice air freshener and a thumbnail-sized picture of an old woman, her angled face confused, its connecting string tangled.

Vitri ducks on the passenger side of the Suburban when the haRd WeaR door opens and a cinder block of a man walks out. Vitri, near the front tire, waits for footsteps the still-sputtering engine won't allow him to hear. So he crouches, further and further. Looks beneath the chassis. Sees toes. Boots. Shins. He angles his arm for a clear shot.

IV.

Idaho will require gasoline. A lot of gasoline. More gasoline than Reyn has, more gasoline than she can stack in the Jeep. She's been wondering what JOHN will demand of her for it. Has been wondering what she can do to JOHN that her mother didn't, or couldn't. Wondering if sex is something that she can think of on the spot, rather than going into it with a scheme, if it's just something she can just feel her way through and improvise as she sees fit. If JOHN will even give her the opportunity to do so. She imagines JOHN inside of her, JOHN trying to talk to her, and she not hearing, not obeying, JOHN becoming angry, JOHN screaming, JOHN punching, JOHN kneeing. Imagines the stout leader not handing off his pistol this time. Imagines going through with it—their insertion, her improvisation, the collective miscommunication—only to be offered enough gasoline to get her back to West Monroe, to her dead mother.

Reyn weaves the Jeep in and out of the same abandoned vehicles on Highway 20, headlights amok in the night, left, then right, then left again. She is a mile from the masked, past SHREVEPORT 14.

Ten minutes or less. That quick. Just shut your eyes and let JOHN spread your legs. Let the fat one in your mouth. Maybe they'll take off their masks, and maybe they'll be gentle, and maybe they'll kiss you, and maybe your first kiss will be okay. Maybe you'll get to Idaho and it'll all be okay.

She spots the first pair of masked eyes half-way-up a tree, inches to the right of the trunk as if peeking from behind. As are the next two, and the two after that. Driving so slow, Reyn watches the eyes vanish in the night, reappearing seconds later, on the ground, as they approach the road, as they form their gauntlet. Closing in, two deep now on each side. She sees the same breasts from before, the same tattoos, the same long-haired boys and girls joining, the masks they'll grow into sliding up, down and across their faces as they walk, yellow hatchets and miniature crowbars sheathed in the belt loops of the denim that has been trimmed to their size.

Beyond the masks to the right, the shelter comes into view. On the lawn now are pallets of wood, piles of shingles. Cans of paint are stacked and partially lit by the same oil lanterns, the same candles on the same stumps. Leaned against the shelter is a motorcycle, its tires off and nearby, accompanied by more tires, by assorted metals, all leaned against stacks of car batteries.

51

Think of gasoline. Think of Idaho. That license plate, those peaks.

JOHN and the fat leader emerge from the structure and walk toward the road. But Reyn does not stop the Jeep. Foot hovering over the brake, she thinks, *They won't negotiate with you. They will yank you out of the Jeep as if you were a doll.* Reyn scans the gauntlet. A boy, maybe four or five years old, takes his place between two older children on the left shoulder of the road. He is the only one not wearing a mask. *They will shred your clothes at the seams. They will let each man have their turn.* The boy's nose is small and flat. His eyes point inward. *They will force you to become them.* Jeep still crawling, she wonders if maybe keeping a mask from his face is punishment. For stealing, maybe, for mouthing off, for not knowing his place. For his deformity. *This will be the end.*

Reyn feels a throb from the back left quarter of the Jeep. A quick bounce, a tiny bounce. A squish. Reyn presses the brake as members of the gauntlet enclose the Jeep. In the driver's side mirror, Reyn watches the masked mob huddle in the red brake light. Between two women struggling for a view, she sees a young girl lying on the pavement, clutching an injured foot, the rest of her body writhing. A hose unkinking itself. Screaming, Reyn knows, in agony. Screaming at Reyn. Screaming because of Reyn.

She feels a thump from the passenger side.

Reyn turns her head. The passenger window has cracked into a spider web, thin divots extending from impact, stretching toward each corner. On the other side of that window, a sinewy woman winds up her yellow crowbar. She delivers another thump. The cracks expand. Faster, thicker. Specks of the crowbar's yellow paint embed themselves in the glass, smear with another thump. And another. The window bends inward.

More join. Men, women, children, with instruments or fists, or both, pound the driver's side window, the back window, the quarter panels, each bumper. One stabs the back right tire, which eases that quarter of the Jeep to the pavement. The thumps are closing in.

Do it.

Press the gas pedal.

The mob in front of the Jeep steps aside when JOHN arrives, translucent in the light, ethereal, yellow ax gripped tight, its handle as long as his torso. He just stands there—three seconds, five seconds, seven—daring Reyn to move.

Do it.

And then JOHN lifts the ax and brings its edge down on the Jeep's hood. In it goes, and in it stays—Reyn, once gathered from her instinctual dodging of the ax's arc, watches JOHN struggle to remove the blade. Both of his hands are on its handle, a foot presumably on the front bumper for leverage. And—this incision, this wound to what for so long now has been her home—it irks Reyn. It offends Reyn. She feels it in her shoulders, in her torso, in her thighs, and shins, and feet.

She presses the gas pedal.

JOHN's face slams onto the Jeep's hood. And off they go down the road, the gauntlet giving chase. When JOHN lifts his head, Reyn sees that the right side of his mask is cracked. One plastic shard is deep into his tan-lined cheek, a slim crimson dash streaking to his neck.

But he hangs on, ax handle palmed, a grip strong enough not to just hold on, but to advance himself up the hood, toward the windshield. Bursts of pistol light fill each mirror. Reyn swerves the Jeep. Thinking it will send JOHN tumbling onto the road, Reyn stomps on the brake. While JOHN slips momentarily, he soon regains his grip, and, through the crack in his mask, gives Reyn the tiniest of smiles, dark lips curling.

I'm sorry.

Reyn presses the gas pedal. Further, harder. The steering wheel shakes in her hands. More pistol light behind her. She jerks the Jeep left, then right. Further, harder. Left again. Right again. Harder. Sharper. And down goes JOHN, pulled beneath the Jeep, legs first, ax still stuck in the hood. Reyn feels the tires climb over his body; sees in her rearview the mob sprinting to its fallen leader.

I'm sorry, I'm sorry, I'm sorry.

V.

Hammer sets a jar of mayonnaise on the barn floor. "Should be able to find a glob in there somewhere," he says. His voice reminds Vitri of a near-empty tube of toothpaste, remnants rolled out from otherwise inaccessible pockets; a battle for words to leave his throat. "You sure you don't want to stay in the house?"

Vitri, scarf over his nose and mouth, back against a barn wall, grabs the jar. "I'll be fine here." The light from his candle reveals blue-grey swirls within the jar.

Hammer pulls a thin, folded magazine from the inside of his jacket. He hands it to Vitri. "Wouldn't want you to feel lonely is all."

Vitri unrolls the magazine. DEEP THROAT is its title. NOVEMBER 2001. A young brunette woman is on the cover, straddling a piano bench, ample lips parted, hands over her nipples.

Hammer backs across the barn aisle and eases his lit candle to the floor, then himself, resting his back against a support beam, then his neck, his asymmetrical chin illuminated—bashed, Vitri immediately knew at the Suburban, by fists, by boot heels; a tetherball for the world.

"My brother used to lock me in here when I was younger," Hammer says. "The first few times he did, he coaxed me in with the promise of a cigarette—one cigarette— or a can of Lone Star—just one—and other things, too, things a twelve-year-old thinks he wants." Hammer takes the double action revolver from his coat—the pistol he says hasn't fired for over a decade—and wiggles it as if to say it too was once a promise. He sets it on the floor, lips curling into something of a grin. "Well, once I figured out that there was no beer, and that there was no cigarette, I put up a fight. Kicked, screamed, even bit him once or twice. But it was no use. He was stronger than I was, plain and simple. He'd kill all the lights, jam a broomstick through the doorhandles. He thought it was funny, I guess." Hammer's grin subsides. He pinches the dry skin from his lips, rolls it into a ball and tosses it on the barn floor. "Dad had already left by then. Mom's mind was on her way out. So here I'd be until morning, on the floor, against that very wall, just listening to them fucking pigs root, snort, screw, squeal. Root, snort, screw, squeal. Jesus. Couldn't ever fall asleep. So I'd hum, I'd talk to them. I'd talk to them fucking pigs."

Vitri has no intention of commenting on Hammer's story, no intention of apologizing for what Hammer was subjected to, no intention of discussing the routines of swine. Nor does he have any intention of pleasuring himself here, in this barn. Vitri does not care. He does not want to care.

"So I know how alone one can feel in here," Hammer says. "That's all."

Yet the compassionate sliver of Vitri cannot overlook the fact that all of it—the magazine, the mayonnaise, the story, the shelter—has been handed over with sincerity, with an honesty someone like Hammer cannot fake.

"Thank you," Vitri says. He lifts the rolled magazine to clarify his gratitude.

"I'm the one that should be thanking you, Freddie."

Vitri hadn't forgotten what he'd told Hammer to call him, but hearing it once more sends his mind into a temporary panic, a race to rediscover the ways in which he's distorted the truth. Freddie: a former police officer born and raised in El Paso. Freddie: not a good enough shot to be a sniper, but for a stretch was sturdy enough to serve as the point man on the department's SWAT team. Freddie: he has been in love before, yes, with many women—"The Rainbow," Vitri told Hammer, meaning: blonde, brunette, raven, redhead, aged grey, and punk green—but has never committed to marriage. Freddie: he has one brother, one sister, both older, both overseas, both, "In one of the Koreas by now." Freddie: father to no one.

Lies. All lies. Lies that somehow led to the untying of his stomach, to licking the bowl of chicken broth Hammer served him on the porch steps, lies that led to a second bowl, lies that led to two separate rounds of vomiting.

"Thanking me for what?" Vitri asks.

"For not killing my dumb ass." A trail of piss had stretched from groin to ankle seconds after Vitri rose from behind the Suburban and took aim. "Can't say I wouldn't have deserved it, leaving it out in the open like that." He chuckles; shakes his head.

Vitri had wanted to pull the trigger. Part of him still wishes he had, that he'd be better off, farther along, that he'd be somewhere in Louisiana by now instead of in this barn, at this farmhouse, with this man. *Take no chances. Eliminate all threats.* It's the mindset he knows his survival hinges upon. The mindset he must adapt.

But Hammer had surrendered immediately, arms like masts in the sky, baggy khaki jacket its sails; that slender nose, bent as if broken and left unset; remaining hair in the shape of a horseshoe, the crown of his head burnt pink and peeling; his eyes— brown, beyond scared, damp—had shrieked that he will forever be incapable of violence. Vitri had felt pity while staring at Hammer. He'd lowered the pistol, shook the man's hand, allowed him to drive, to speak as if they were destined to be friends from the start.

"I just hope haRd WeaR gets some foot traffic soon," Vitri says.

As Hammer had told it, when he's able to siphon enough gas to do so, he drives around and searches scrapyards and abandoned strip malls to stock haRd WeaR, his first and only entrepreneurial endeavor. Some days, he can't even find a washer; other days, it's like a scrounger's jackpot—pocketfuls of nails and drill bits, claw hammers and screwdrivers secured in his belt loops. He has stumbled upon handsaws, upon wrenches of all sizes and colors, sometimes even an entire set. Rasps, utility belts, a plethora of chisels. Which was, at least for a moment, enough for Vitri to look at Hammer with the slightest bit of admiration, for it was he, finding the confidence after everyone else's had been stolen from them like hotel towels, that was looking to the future with hope, and doing something about it.

"Me too," Hammer says. "Has to. Me and Mom are getting low on everything."

"I thought you said your mom was gone." The sun had set by the time they'd arrived; the farmhouse completely dark. Outside of their footsteps on the porch, there'd been no movement whatsoever.

"*Dad* is gone. Dad *has been* gone. Mom's just batshit crazy." Hammer reels in his laugh. "I love her. I mean that. Really do. If you ask me, though—" He pauses, leans in as if his mother were nearby, ear to the barn door, then whispers, "It's a goddamn curse." He leans back. "I'm tellin' you, Freddie, you're lucky to not have any family in a time like this. Don't have to wipe no asses, don't have no one you have to share your food with. Free to wander as you damn well please."

Vitri lets that sink in. Digests it. Lets it tumble to his gut. Can see Hammer's point, can even align it with the views of a much-younger version of himself. But he doesn't agree. Freedom and mobility, Vitri believes, are separate. Freedom, not mobility, is confusion, in having so many choices, too many choices. Freedom, not mobility, is fear in choosing the wrong place, the wrong person, the wrong route. Freedom, not mobility, is an agent of restriction, immobility a byproduct.

"Mmhmm," Vitri says. It is all he intends to say. He believes his thoughts to be over Hammer's head, and is left to wonder whether Hammer's statement would've been different had he told him the truth, that he'd had a wife and son, that his wife put a bullet in the boy's head, and then her own.

"Tell me, though," Hammer says. He settles in, crosses his stiff legs, candlelight swiveling as he does so, shedding light on the oblong scar along his neck, a discolored oval inches beneath his right jaw. "You said you've been in love, and with several women. What—what does—" Hammer pauses, gathers himself. "What does that feel like?"

The question both stuns and flatters Vitri. Stuns him because, despite Hammer's unattractiveness, he would've expected love to surface and be fulfilled somewhere in his thirty-odd years. An obese woman at some convenience store. An anorexic woman with scars on her wrists the shape of razor blades. A pig in this very barn. It flatters him not just because Hammer has, as coyly as an ungraceful man like Hammer can, asked for guidance through memories, but that, within hours of having Vitri's 9mm aimed at his face, Hammer believes Vitri to be the man to ask. Hammer believes Freddie to be the man to ask. Thin armor peeled off. Guard down. A desire to connect.

"It's hard to explain," Vitri says.

"Mmhmm."

Vitri stares at Hammer. Fragile. Fractured. Curious. *Something*. He needs to say something. "It can be great."

Another, "Mmhmm." A nod. *Go on*, it says, *go on*.

"So many things need to align for it to last, though. The moon, the stars, the money. You need to be assertive. You need to be sensitive. You need to stay home. You need to go places, keep things in motion." Vitri pauses. "In order for love to be great, you need to give them the world."

"That sounds exhausting," Hammer says.

"It is," Vitri says. "It really is." And he is in a trance, lost in a memory, eyes fixed on a support beam in shadow, a dozen feet or so from Hammer. He slips off his scarf. "Sometimes you do wonder if it's all worth it, the effort, but then there are other times—as brief as they are—where those questions just go away."

"Tell me—," Hammer says, realizing that his listener's stare is elsewhere.

Vitri is on a boat. His wife is twenty feet away. "I remember watching her walk across that deck. Strapless white dress. No, wait. Red dress. Scarlet, maroon, I don't know. But I remember thinking that she looked so beautiful, and I remember feeling so proud, so fucking proud, of her, of me, for somehow finding the balls to pursue, for taking a risk and actually having it pay off." Her hands are in his. "And for having the opportunity to look back and think of how great it'd been, to look forward and not be scared." Vitri leans in, smells her hair, memory tricking him into its scent being of almonds. "I wasn't on the river that trip. I was somewhere between it, and the sun. Trees, clouds, mountains, I didn't care. Everything she said. Everything she did. It was perfect."

"Mmhmm," Hammer says. He stares. "Brunette?"

"Blonde. Straight blonde hair. Legs for days. And her shoulders—there was something about her shoulders that I loved. They were broad, but not too broad, you know? Sturdy, strong, but also very feminine." Vitri smiles again, thinking of the way his wife's skin would tense and rise when he'd graze her shoulders with his finger.

"How good of a fuck was she?" Hammer asks.

Which jars Vitri. His eyes shift. He sits up. Scratches his beard. Feels *How good of a fuck was she?* ping-ponging from ear to ear. Squints at Hammer. "What was that?"

"I asked how good of a fuck she was," Hammer says. "You said she was blonde. You said she had long legs. Those broad shoulders. Sounds to me like she was built to fuck." Awaiting an answer, Hammer watches Vitri closely. Notices his eyes drifting back to the floor. Notices his twirling thumbs. Notices the elongated silence. "I was just curious, Freddie, that's all. Don't feel like you need to—"

"She was good," Vitri interrupts, eyes astray. "She was very good."

Hammer isn't sure of his place here, whether or not his best route is to ask more questions, or to let Vitri's statements stand as they do. All he finds himself doing is watching Vitri—eyes are fixed, thumbs no longer twirling, but playing their role in the pinching of the scarf, in the dragging of its frayed edges back over his mouth and nose.

"Big tits? Big ass?" Vitri asks, voice muffled now. "No. Neither. They were decent. Decent, yeah. Enough to have fun with, sure—plenty of fun—but what set her off is the kind of shit she'd ask me to do to her."

"She wanted it rough?"

"She did. Liked it from every angle. Liked it in every hole." Vitri looks at Hammer. "Powerless. She liked to feel powerless."

The Jeep is at the bottom of the hill, on its side, ax still in the hood, its circulatory system still emptying—a stream of fluid, oil, and gas obeying the slope, running to the river below. Because the left headlight has been smashed, a lone beam of light shines on the tree stumps that brought the sliding Jeep to a halt.

Reyn walks to the highway, eyes wide but vision still blurred, spinning, swooping. Hair clings to the blood smeared on her left cheek. She'd felt the rest of the tires go, she'd felt the Jeep lower. She'd seen the sparks. As to what had happened next, she can't be certain. Though the road thus far doesn't reveal such a scenario, she may have flipped soon after and skidded the rest of the way. She may have even centered the immediate swerve, only to lose the battle later, when the pull had become too much for her tired hands to correct. She walks on. Stops. Fifty yards from where she'd crested the hill are short and narrow rubber strips, consecutively spaced three feet from one another. They span the width of the road, the only way for vehicles to emerge unscathed being the slopes. Reyn crouches, examines the strips. Each long nail, from point to strip painted red. She pinches the rubber between her fingers and attempts to lift one of the strips but to no avail. Adhered to the asphalt.

She then stands and begins her trek back to the Jeep, certain that the site will soon swarm with the masked. Not in the next five minutes, or ten, or even thirty. But soon. She pictures dozens of them sprinting toward her, dozens that followed her on foot all this way, the ten or so miles she'd traveled, dozens with pointed weapons meant for her, to pierce her feet, her sternum, her throat. She stumbles back down the hill to extract what she can from the wreckage.

VII.

"She likes her car rides, tell you what," Hammer says for the third time. He smiles as he slows the Suburban to a crawl, passing exit ramps blocked off by accordioned semi-trucks. "Isn't that right, Ma?"

Hammer's mother moans from the backseat. For this trip, he'd blotched makeup across his mother's face. He'd situated her in a deep purple top and semi-clean jeans. He'd forced antique earrings into years-closed holes but had forgotten to wipe the blood from her lobes.

Vitri watches the frail lady in the passenger side mirror, her mouth agape, grey hair jutting every which way, like a ship captain's wheel. For the third time, he obliges and says through his scarf: "You always take her with you?"

"Can't leave her at the house when there are people like you roaming around." For the first time, Hammer shoves Vitri's shoulder as if they are old pals, then lets out a laugh, deep and haughty.

Which, more than anything else, depresses Vitri. He is to be in this Suburban until Shreveport, with the old woman that has been doused in rank perfume, with this giddy Hammer, this guard-entirely-down Hammer, this Hammer that has emerged from the cocoon that his self-doubt had spun.

"Have to admit, this is exciting for me. See, I was gonna be like you," Hammer says, "before everything went to hell. Just pack all my shit up and head north, to Michigan, to Minnesota, somewhere like that. Thought about it a lot."

"What's stopping you from going now?"

"You saw me piss myself," Hammer says. He shrugs. "I'm a pussy. I found that out real fast. You should've seen when everything went dark. Didn't leave the house. Sat in my room, wishing that, if this was it, if this was how the world was gonna end, that I'd somehow be the first to go, that somehow God would seek me out, and only me, and make it quick—"

"Mmhmm."

"—I even told myself that it was okay to leave Mom here to die. Said to myself that it was her time, that it'd been her time, all the bullshit we tell ourselves about death." Hammer glances at the rearview mirror, at its reflection of the woman in back. "But I

64

didn't go anywhere. Stayed. Watched the vehicles zoom by. Watched the leaves fall. Watched all the crops shrivel up like a cold nutsack." Hammer sighs. "The day I heard the planes was, well, that was it. That was when I decided for good that I wasn't going anywhere. That I wasn't suited for the risk."

Vitri leans forward. Looks at Hammer. "Planes?" The last plane Vitri had seen was a commercial airliner, miles up, its contrail slashing across a clear sky. Days after the blackout.

"Yeah, planes."

"How long ago?"

"How long ago did I hear them?"

"Yeah."

"A couple weeks. Maybe three. You haven't heard 'em?" Hammer watches Vitri shake his head no. "Huh."

Silence.

"You really haven't heard them at all?"

"Who's flying them?"

"Fuck if I know," Hammer says. "Military, maybe."

"Whose?"

"Ours, Argentina's, Kazakhstan's, does it matter?"

"Jets?"

"No, no, hell no. Jesus, slow down a bit, would you? They're old cargo planes and crop dusters. Dusters have been dropping shit for months now. Pesticides, insecticides, rodenticides, all kinds of cides. No way you didn't smell it on the way over."

Vitri thinks of the fields he walked past yesterday, of the cattle, of walking to Florida drenched in chemicals, of coughing out organs. He thinks of flesh sliding from his skeleton.

"What about Florida?" Vitri asks. "Do you think they're dropping anything there?"

Hammer chuckles. "Nothing else to kill here."

The Suburban rumbles east.

"I was what they'd call a good kid," Hammer says. "With all those promises my dipshit brother made, I didn't even take my first sip of beer until I was twenty-three years old. Twenty-three!"

Vitri leans his head against the passenger window. Fields upon fields upon fields. The occasional giant tree dying. A paint-stripped home here and there, siding as grey as the overcast sky.

There are no planes.

"Mmhmm," Vitri says.

Not in Texas, not in Louisiana, not in Florida.

"That's no joke, either. And, just my luck, the whole world goes to shit by the time my palate declares that any sort of alcohol actually tastes good."

He opened a store when there are no customers. He pissed himself at the sight of you.

"I'd have to say that my favorite was this one that they call a hefeweizen. That wasn't the brand; it was the type of beer, you see. And they didn't sell it in bottles either, at least not this kind. You'd have to go to a bar, and I don't mean one of the oil rig bars, I mean an upscale place, a trimmed beard and eyeglasses type of place."

He gave you mayonnaise to stroke your dick. He carries a pistol that doesn't fire. He dolls up his dying mother.

"Were you a beer man, Freddie?"

Hammer is wrong.

"Freddie?"

"Whiskey." *Hammer doesn't know a fucking thing.* "I liked whiskey."

Clouds are yanked spaceward by an invisible puppeteer, their remains rallying into nothing but thumbprints. To the north is rain, a mauve wave hovering over the distant treelines.

Vitri props his scarved face with his elbow and hand.

"And then I had these two cousins. On her side," Hammer points to his mother. "Melvin and Marvin—we called Melvin 'Haha,' and Marvin 'Giggles'—anyway, they were, as you can probably tell by their nicknames, of the prankster mold. Little hellions that couldn't tiptoe that line schools draw in the sand and label, 'suitable'. I mean, you probably know the type, being an officer of the law and all."

There are no police officers. There are no courts. There are no jails.

"Well, one day, the two of them—they were inseparable, let me tell you—well, one day, they, without telling anyone, decided to drop out of high school. Waited until the day Marvin turned eighteen and just up and quit. Said fuck it all. Didn't go anymore." Hammer pauses, glances at Vitri. "You wanna know where they went? You wanna know what they were up to?"

There are no judges. There are no consequences.

"Huh? Do you?"

The Suburban comes to a screeching halt, just before an overpass. Its brake lights shut off; its engine stays on. There are no screams. No sound at all until the driver's side door opens and onto the highway steps Hammer, arms raised. He stares through the open door. Says nothing.

"Get her the fuck out of here," Vitri says from within the Suburban.

Hammer listens. Hurries to the back door, opens it and lifts his mother out, pivoting his body so that her legs don't nick the vehicle.

The passenger door opens. Closes. Circling around the front of the Suburban is Vitri, 9mm drawn and aimed at Hammer and his mother.

Hammer backs away.

Vitri shuts the back door and, without another word, climbs into the driver's seat. Shuts the door. Takes off.

East he goes, 9mm still in his hand, east, east, east. He glances once more at the rearview mirror, at himself, at the twirling picture of Hammer's mother. He sets the 9mm on the passenger seat. Tugs the picture and its string off. Rolls down the driver's side window. Tosses it out. Leaves the window open, leaves the rearview at a severe angle.

A treeline north of the highway. A treeline south. From one to the other—blocking the highway, blocking each shoulder—are tree trunks and telephone poles, stacked eight feet high, all of which have been paint-brushed vermilion.

The Suburban approaches. Stops. Vitri steps onto the highway. He walks north along the stack. He walks south and eventually comes back to the center once he sees there is no way he can maneuver the vehicle around or over. For a moment, Vitri puts his hands on the wood. Tries pushing the stack. He pushes, and pushes, and pushes, grunting as he does so, the pushes soon becoming punches, the grunting soon becoming screams. Once exhausted, he turns around. Looks west.

And then he walks back to the Suburban, to the passenger side. He pulls out his backpack and slings it over his shoulders as he walks around the stack, leaving Hammer's truck for the taking.

From the hill where Vitri stands, Shreveport is in view, mustard-colored land risen like dough around its outskirts, buildings tall, robust from this distance. The air smells of sulfur. Potent. Seeping through the scarf, stinging Vitri's nostrils. With watery eyes he looks to the sky to see three sickly crows circling, obsidian feathers descending, casualties of their battle with the swirling wind.

On the tree stump goes the box of matches, the .22 pistol, the bar of soap. Vitri finds the can of soup he was looking for in the bottom of his backpack. He removes the lid he'd rubber-banded shut and, still standing, takes one brief, calculated sip. It tastes as advertised: like expired tomatoes. His tastebuds don't fight it, though, nor does his stomach. All the sip seems to do is make Vitri hungrier. He finds himself craving a salad. Spinach leaves and halved olives, garlic-doused croutons and feta cheese, the tomatoes diced and smothered in the Greek dressing his wife fought to keep out of the house.

He takes another sip. Thinks of bacon, and melted sharp cheddar cheese, and wheat bread, a slice or two of tomato somewhere between. Then, pork altogether. And chicken. And beef. Meat he'd marinate overnight and flip on the grill the following afternoon. He takes another sip and misses the farmer's market sweet corn his wife would shuck and season, the green beans, the cauliflower and broccoli. He remembers cooking with her, the graceful routine they'd perform in the kitchen, pans in hand, swiveling around one another to open drawers and cupboard doors, lifting, dicing, mixing, shaking, exchanging smiles in one of the few moments between them where verbal inquiries were unnecessary in knowing what the other thought or desired.

He then thinks of noodles. Big noodles, fat noodles, wheat noodles, white noodles, noodles slathered in tomato sauce. *Nowhere else but Tallahassee.* Vitri stretches the rubber band from the lid to the bottom of the can, then places the can back into his backpack, forming a mound of support around it to prevent tipping and spilling. He stands, places the remaining items into the backpack, zips it shut, then walks down the hill.

Vitri walks through Broadmoor Terrace, the 9mm in hand. Within the subdivision are abandoned but still-gaudy homes whose front lawns house sumacs and cedars barely toting their leaves and needles. Around the homes are shriveled yet still colorful beds of transplanted wildflowers, petals fortunate enough to have consistent shade still pink and purple and white. *Homes of attorneys,* Vitri thinks, *officials, angel investors, physicians.* One—the same home with street-facing windows the height of hunting shacks—has three marble pillars extending from ground to roof. The next has a secluded walkway to a guesthouse larger than what the majority of Waco had called home. Two more down is a ransacked backyard greenhouse, its protective mesh torn, wilted stems drooped over clay pots. Oddly, as if homeowners were still lobbying for a local politician, draped over each garage door are solid red banners, twitching in the wind.

Entering what he may have once considered downtown, Vitri clings to the shadows. When he can't, he carefully moves at a quicker pace, something closer to a crouched jog than to a walk, using parked cars as cover. There's just too much to stand still for. Countless windows, countless buildings, countless doors, a plethora of streets. The city itself is decaying but, unlike Waco, it has yet to be thrashed. Parking meters haven't been uprooted. Bicycle racks, though vacant, remain upright. Flagpoles are bare and bent, but not down. Brick buildings aren't charred, bulldozed to rubble, or left impaled by crane arms. First and second story office windows have only faint fractures, all glass higher intact and tinted.

Before and during the crossing of the intersection nearest the shopping district, Vitri performs a three-sixty turn, arms and eyes fixed, both hands on the 9mm, soon passing a shoe store, a sporting goods store, a lamp store, two thrift stores, then two bookstores and a furniture store, stores, stores, stores. He slows his pace when passing a clothing store—not because of the wadded jackets on the back counter, nor the navy blue briefcase leaned against the wall, but—because of its empty hangers, the shelves on their sides, the vacant S hooks, the tipped racks, the stripped mannequins. He thinks of how his wife and Carmen came in one day, before she on a whim moved east. How his wife leaned on the counter and flirted with him, how Carmen, arms crossed, walked around the store alone, critical eyes behind polarized sunglasses. He remembers how she approached the counter, interrupted, took off her sunglasses, looked at him, and said, "You're in the wrong century here." He remembers her suggestions for optimizing the displays for the store's steady foot traffic—the jackets up front to be nearer to the back, the fedora and bowler displays not only to be updated, but to be swapped, from one side of the store to the other. He remembers ignoring her at first. Remembers voicing to his wife that Carmen didn't know shit. Remembers how over time it ate away at him, standing at that counter, imagining a new layout, imagining *her* layout. Remembers how he walked around the counter, went outside, stood on the sidewalk, looked in through the glass, and thought: *Goddammit, she's right.*

Vitri examines the damage of the store before him now and cannot deny that more than an inkling of him wants to walk inside, wave some sort of wand, and take the first steps toward rehabilitation. The thought halts him, drops his arms, even, the prospect of erecting those shelves, of buffering the hardwood floors, of tagging armfuls of clothes and overloading each hook, bowing each rack. What jolts him from this thought is—

—sounds: distant; southeast; approaching. Clanks of metal. Metal on metal. Glass on metal. Thuds, pings, items shifting.

And footsteps.

Vitri takes cover behind an aluminum garbage can still bungee-corded to a lamppost. He peeks over its rim, at the crosswalk.

Clank. Thud. Ping. Louder now. Nearer.

Vitri readies the 9mm to fire. Glances back over the garbage can. Holds.

Holds.

And holds, until one block from where he crouches, there is a girl. An unarmed girl no older than fifteen, in loose jeans and a purple sweatshirt, with dried blood across her face. In the middle of the road, walking north. Just walking, casually spinning to check her surroundings, wisps of light brown hair latching to the backpack she holds tight to her shoulders. She does not see him. Fails to even glance his direction. Nor does she seem to care at all just how loud she is, how insecure the items are within that backpack. Which should mean nothing to Vitri. Neither her bloody face nor her ignorance should concern him at all. He does not know her. She has not seen him. And those should be the only things that matter.

Yet Vitri finds himself wanting to stand, to say something, to walk to her, grab her shoulder, turn her around, and say, "You're being too loud," or, "Stop," or, "Go home." But soon she is out of Vitri's sight, through the intersection, her noise trapped between northern buildings, clanks and pings faintly echoing.

Vitri rises from his crouch. His eyes stay east, until, in partial shadow, he sees a wooden door open. Out pour two red-masked men, facing west, facing him. Vitri crouches behind the garbage can once more. He expects to hear voices, but there are only footsteps, ascending into a jarring series of sandal slaps on the asphalt.

Vitri peers around the garbage can to see the lead man—the thinner of the two—turn north where the girl did. He is shirtless, toned, and with, from this distance, either scabs or tattoos cradling his shoulder blades. In his right hand is a spiked club the length of Vitri's forearm. Limping behind is a bull of a man in a too-tight red t-shirt, gripping a rusted machete. Only when he turns north does Vitri stand, both hands on his pistol.

South, he thinks. *Go south. They are occupied. Go south. You do not know this girl. You do not need to help this girl. Go south. Go south.*

###

Reyn's forehead skids across the pavement. Her left cheek, her shoulder. Within seconds, she is being flipped onto her back by a lean man in a red bandit mask, his mouth exposed. His bare torso houses scars of various sizes and lengths, some as wide as piano keys, others long and slim, from nipple to abdomen. He climbs atop her and cinches her torso with his knees. Tighter, tighter. Tighter. Reyn jerks, squirms, blood darting down her cheek as she attempts to wriggle her hips free. In retaliation, the man raises his hand, that spiked club. He shouts at her:

"Stop   you   cunt!"

Reyn looks to her right: a vehicle, loose papers, torn cardboard boxes, a gouged brick building, frozen in atrophy. To her left: a shorter man in a red welder's mask walks alongside her and stands. Grips a machete. Massages his left leg with his free hand.

The bandit atop her shouts—she feels it, his voice a series of tremors transferred from his thighs to her ribs. Sharp. Shrill. He tightens his knees' grip even further, until Reyn's breathing becomes labored. Then he hunches over, brings his face close to Reyn's, wispy grey chin whiskers inches from her. Speaks slower.

"   you don't shut up,   your tongue out.   understand me?" He turns to the welder. They speak. They exchange weapons.

Don't let them bind you, Reyn thinks.. *Don't let them drag you along this road. Make sure they kill you here.*

Reyn kicks her feet. Short kicks, furious kicks. She throws her fists at the bandit's arms, his shoulders and chest. She shakes her head; blood from her cheek lands on the bandit's bare chest. She tries to scream, to cry, but can't tell if the vibration she feels is from her or if it is from him—his open mouth, his taut neck says that he is shouting again. Quick commands, indecipherable commands, at her, at the welder. He punches Reyn's mouth with his left hand. She stops. Tongues a loose molar. Gathers. Then she's at it again, kicking, flailing, contorting her body, searching for any sort of gap to exploit.

The welder drops his spiked club, limps over, and eases his way to the asphalt. Once down, he grip's Reyn's forearms and extends them over her head. Pries open each of her hands. Sets his left knee on her left palm. Right on right. Anchors her to the pavement.

Reyn continues to kick, to push, to pull. She even tries to bite the man's stained hands as he grips her head, as he places his thumbs on her upper lip and presses. Sharp pain shoots through Reyn's gums, refocusing her attention, yet intensifying her efforts—pushing, pulling, wiggling, her outstretched shoulders feeling as if they will soon separate from her body.

The shirtless man grabs her chin. Redirects her eyes. "Open. Your. Mouth."

No.

Despite her outstretched shoulders feeling as if they will soon separate from her body, Reyn fights. Somehow frees her mouth from the heavier man's grip and snags one of his finger within her teeth. Clamps down. Closes her lips tight and intends to keep them that way, no matter what.

Do it already. Kill me here.

She sees it coming, the welder's wound fist. And she can do nothing to dodge it. He connects with her right cheek. Once, twice. And she is dazed, spinning, her pulse reverberating within her temples. That same fist uncoils itself and reaches into Reyn's mouth, hooking its fingers to her lower lip. Left hand: upper lip. Together they pry open her mouth and, as the spinning slows, Reyn can see the bandit atop her move his hand to the back of the machete blade, near the tip. Even with so little room, he reaches into Reyn's mouth and grabs her tongue. He begins to cut. And it begins to gush. Bound to gravity, obeying its every rule, to the back of her throat the blood goes, more and more as he saws, and saws, and saws. There's too much; she can't swallow all this blood.

73

But she tries, again and again, and can only cough. Her head jerks out of the his hands; blood spatters across the bandit's face.

The bandit backs away. Wipes his face. And she is being punched again. Two, three, four times, both sides of her head, both cheeks. Her vision begins to fade, to distort, to swirl into an oil painting over an open flame. More blood pools in her throat. She can feel her bones resetting.

And then the welder's knees roll off of her palms. The bandit goes limp, falls forward, his chest sliding onto and across her face, smearing blood into her eyes, into her hair. She cannot see, cannot breathe, cannot help but panic—flail, and tug, and somehow worm out from beneath the bandit's dead weight, only to emerge near the welder, curled on the road, hugging his stomach.

Reyn tries to stand, but falls, her brain unable to will her weak legs to do so. She tries again and falls. Once more. And then someone—some hand—grabs her. A large hand, a moist hand, a man's hand. In feeling those fingers, in assuming them to belong to yet another red mask, Reyn wriggles free, until that same hand grabs the back of her sweatshirt and lifts her to her feet. She's turned around. Though her eyes are addled, she, as the man lifts his hands to remove the scarf around his mouth, sees that he has a pistol in his hand.

Run, go, run, run.

Scarf down, he grabs her wrist. Holds her still. But she fights him. Chops at his forearm, strikes his elbow.

He steps closer. Holds her steady. "Can you   " When she does not respond, he wipes her eyes with the back of his free hand. "Can. You. Walk?"

Once more, Reyn fights. She chops. Yanks. Strikes his hands from her. Free, she steps and steps, traveling only five or six feet before wobbling left, then right. The man hurries to Reyn's side, places his arm around her shoulders and, together, they walk south, past the bandit, who lies face down on the pavement. Feet away, the welder twists in pain. He points at the sky, at the buildings, at his stomach, at Reyn. Lifts his mask. One chalky eye, film over a blue iris, the other brown, and angry. Spit flies from his lips and tongue. Reyn feels her ears being covered by the man's hands and—

—Reyn is on her knees, vomiting blood onto the sidewalk. No chunks, just small pools of red under the sun. Though her hair is being pulled back she can see that the tips have become paintbrushes, dipped in red, and—

—They are in the shade, under a large green and white awning. The man has leaned her against a brick building and is now gently opening her mouth, his eyes squinted for examination—

—Reyn is flexed over the man's shoulder, head down, stomach spiraling as her eyes try to keep pace with his feet. She tries to lift her head, to see what he is walking them toward, but can only go so high before the throb takes over, relegating her instead to watching blood string from her mouth to his shoulders, to watching sweat run down his neck. There are strands of gray in the man's otherwise black beard. His nose is long and aquiline, cheekbones pronounced—

—Reyn is in an alley. Feet from her, the man kicks a door. He kicks again. And again. Then he stops. Readjusts the scarf around his mouth. Looks at Reyn. Backs away from the door to catch his breath. Then he is kicking again. Reyn reaches her arm toward him but cannot raise it past her ribcage. *Stop. They'll find us. Just stop.* She looks at her hands, then—

—Reyn is on a concrete floor. To her right is a tipped metal trashcan steadied by stacked bricks. There is a fire within the trashcan and, other than its immediate glow, the room is dark, nearer to purple than to black, quilts hung improperly over the windows and letting in slices of yellow-orange light. Loveseats are illuminated, recliners, dining tables that have been pressed against those quilts, against doors.

What the flame consumes, Reyn cannot tell, though near the trashcan is a pile of rotting wood, a pile of rug remnants, a pile of TIME. Atop is the bundle of syringes. Most of them have been damaged, guts exposed to air, hardened to the plastic. Reyn looks at the trashcan. Resting in the flame is a the point of a four-inch blade. To her left is a mound of bloodstained Q-tips, an open bottle of water, an open bottle of rubbing alcohol. The man, however, is nowhere to be seen. He doesn't weave between the furniture. He doesn't tend the fire. *Gone*, Reyn thinks. *He's gone. You aren't hurt. Time to stand.*

Reyn tries. Tumbles. And, in doing so, knocks over the bottles, their contents converging on the concrete. When she turns herself over, there the man is, a silhouette in the nearest corner, a white rectangle snug in his arm as he shuts a desk drawer and climbs over its surface. Outside of the fire's glow, his face looks so dark, his beard so full, his teeth so white. Her blood is all over his clothes, all over that scarf.

Reyn tries to stand once more. Tumbles into his arms. The man eases her back to the concrete. He watches her. Says something. Says it again. Leans in closer, says it once more, directly in front of her.

"You O.K.?"

She isn't. The throb is still there, on her tongue, in her cheekbones. Her skull feels like a tightening spring, fixed to burst through flesh at any second. She wants to go home. Crawl onto her bed, shape the covers around her body. She wants to go to the Jeep. She wants to go to her mother.

"You O.K.?"

Reyn stares at him. Nods.

He nods. Says something, lips too quick for her to read. Grabs the topmost issue of TIME, rips its pages, tosses them into the flame. Another issue. More tearing. Another.

Reyn reaches for him. Blood spills over her bottom lip. *Stop*, she thinks. *Stop.*

He puts down her arm, then he starts in on the syringes, chucking them one by one into the trashcan. The flame intensifies, leaps sideways. Turns pink-then-red-then-purple-then-blue, contents digested in a matter of seconds. When the flame settles, the man reaches for the bottle of water and, on his knees, swivels toward Reyn. He motions for her to open her mouth. She does. He pours. Motions for her to spit. She does. He then exchanges the water for the rubbing alcohol. Repeat.

"You O.K.?"

76

She waits for the burn of the alcohol to pass. Allows the tears down her cheeks. Nods.

The man nods. And, in one fluid motion, he drops the plastic bottle and stretches to grab the knife from the trashcan. Without warning, he grabs Reyn's chin and, despite her combatting it, brings her face close. He turns his left fist sideways and wedges it between her teeth. Accepts her bite. He accepts it, grimaces, and eases the hot blade in. Presses it to the side of Reyn's wounded tongue.

Upon the staircase, Vitri listens once more to the small engine that has been intermittently touring Shreveport for an hour now. The first time he heard it, Vitri hustled up the staircase on the opposite side of this former furniture store, to a window not yet boarded, and peered out into the night, locating within seconds the bike's lone beam of light. Wandering, scouting, lingering in a way that almost seemed sad. The second time Vitri heard the engine, he jogged to the exact same spot and observed the exact same thing. Now, chin to chest, he waits on *this* staircase, more annoyed than anything else, at the interruption, yes, but also at the respect he must give the sound— despite slim odds of that dirt bike approaching this very building, its rider dismounting and somehow on their own, in the dark, finding their way inside, the question of *What if?* has burrowed, bounced around, and continued to go unanswered.

He sighs as he, with the scarf over his right hand, re-grips the warm lip of the trashcan and moves it in an abbreviated circular motion, stoking flakes of ash to orange at its bottom, a quiet action performed to busy the mind, to delay looking inward for an answer. Part of him would like to believe that he'd drop the trashcan, sprint the staircase, draw his 9mm and once more protect the girl. Another part of him hopes he'd, yes, leave this trashcan here, and, yes, sprint up that staircase, blow out the lone candle he'd left lit in the second story showroom, avoid conflict altogether, and just hide with the girl; just hide, and hope. The last part of him views this entire afternoon as a waste. A burden, that's what this part of Vitri sees the girl as, someone he'd stupidly exhausted resources on. Someone that could be dead within the hour. *South*, he thinks now, listening to the engine become distant. *South, south, south.* Up the stairs he goes.

The showroom is small, twelve by twelve at best, with ten-foot ceilings. As Vitri enters he again looks at the torn maritime-themed wallpaper and wonders if it once represented a child's bedroom, the gold anchors and white sails something for a cribbed infant to stare at, to misunderstand and reach for. He pictures sea blue nightstands, and paintings of schooners, miniature yawls and sloops. He pictures cruise ship bunk beds pressed against the north wall, top bunk and its view of the city below through the three casement windows something to be bickered over by children forced along on a Sunday afternoon, children who moments prior worked as a team to spring themselves from their parents and the endless first-floor testing of office chairs and bedsprings. He pictures the room alive, warm with foot traffic, not cold and gutted, as it is now, save for end tables whose legs Vitri has snapped and piled. Save for the bloodied girl at its center.

Vitri sets the trashcan in the doorway, near the candle he'd lit and placed as far from the window as possible. He quietly feeds two more table legs to the dying flame, then wads of TIME. Watches the varnish sizzle off; listens to the wood pop; runs his index finger over the candle wax that has solidified on the hardwood floor; runs the same finger through the candle's flame. Walks to the girl. Stares.

Her right cheek looks like a halved blood orange, outer ring thin and bright, interior dark and risen. Right eye swollen, brow and lash crusted red. The last time he checked her tongue was over an hour ago, before he'd secured each door downstairs. As for how it will heal, if he'd truly sealed the wound, or if it'll reopen hours from now when she tries to speak, Vitri hasn't a clue.

The girl rolls onto her back, her blood-crusted left hand finding and settling upon Vitri's boot. Vitri crouches. Feels the notebook shift in his waistband. Unwraps the scarf from his hand so that he can grab hers. Moves it closer to her stomach. Rolls her back to her side, so that, should that seal break, she won't drown in her blood.

"Get some rest," he whispers into her ear.

Vitri walks to the right side of the casement windows and inches his face between the chilled glass and the quilt he rigged over it with wire. The sun is rising, hues of orange and pink evolving, from mere rays to slices. He used to love seeing cities in shadow. It once made him feel as if playing fields were leveled, however brief, however fleeting, just long enough to look at a skyscraper and see only a rectangle, long enough to read the names etched on front doors and not resentfully picture their lives for the sake of comparing it to his own, long enough to breathe and not feel as if doing so brought anyone pain, not him, not his wife, not his son. Sunrises once brought him peace. But now, all it brings is strain. Over which part of him is right. Over what this day will look like, or the next, or the next, whether they'll be dictated by him and how far his feet will allow him to go, or by the girl on the floor—

There it is again, the bike. Distant, idling somewhere in the blue-grey below. Vitri walks left, along the window. Stares north until, four blocks out, he spots one brake light, one headlight aimed at a white brick building. While from this distance, from this height, the bike's operator is featureless, he or she dismounts without panic and proceeds to kill the engine. Gone are the lights. Gone is the rider.

Vitri stays at the window. Thirty seconds. One minute, two minutes. He remains long enough for the sun to reject his assumption: the bike is yellow, not red. A scavenger doing what that part of him feels he too should be doing: stashing as much as possible for the journey ahead.

DON'T SPEAK. JUST READ. IF YOU CAN, WRITE.

THAT CUT ON YOUR TONGUE IS DEEP. COULD TEAR AND GUSH AGAIN. DON'T SWALLOW ANY MORE BLOOD IF YOU CAN HELP IT, THOUGH. WHEN YOU'RE ABLE, SWISH SOME MORE ALCOHOL AROUND YOUR MOUTH. WILL BURN BUT WILL HELP HEAL.

WE'RE ON THE SECOND FLOOR. NEEDED HIGHER GROUND. FOURTH WAS TOO HIGH, BUT I'LL SHOW YOU THE VIEW, IF YOU'D LIKE. ALL IS QUIET FOR NOW.

I HAVE SOUP FOR YOU WHEN YOU'RE READY.

VITRI

REYN
I LIKE THAT
I LIKE VITRI
HOW'S THE SOUP?
GOOD. DOES YOUR HAND HURT?
YEAH
I'M SORRY
DON'T BE
I AM
YOU HEAR THAT?
YEAH

X	O	X
O	O	X
X	X	O

WHERE YOU HEADED?
I DON'T KNOW
YOU DON'T KNOW?
IDAHO
FAMILY?
FATHER
ALIVE?
MAYBE
MOTHER?
DEAD
I'M SORRY
WHERE YOU HEADED?
TALLAHASSEE
WHY?
COUSIN
ONLY FAMILY?
HE'S SAILING TO SAN JUAN
NEVER BEEN
ME EITHER
JUST YOUR COUSIN?
DON'T KNOW
WHEN?
A FEW DAYS
NEVER COMING BACK?
NEVER

HOW MANY PEOPLE?
DON'T KNOW
ROOM FOR ME?
MAYBE
I CAN'T STAY HERE
NO, YOU CAN'T
CAN I GO WITH YOU?
MORE SUPPLIES
I CAN HELP
STAY. REST
O.K.
DON'T LET THE FIRE DIE OUT
O.K.

###

There is something beyond the concealment of Vitri's lips that makes Reyn uneasy about that scarf, how its placement renders him featureless—gone is his gently aging beard, hidden are his high and weathered cheekbones, transformed are his eyes, the burgundy fabric somehow extracting shades of deep brown from their centers, layered instead in bright paranoia. Even his posture changes with the scarf on. Shoulders back, spine straight, weight shifted from his heels to the balls of his feet. Ready to pounce, Reyn tells herself, ready to sprint from her and back into the world. Why wouldn't he? Why not run? Because of her he has been stuck here, in this building, not making his way to Tallahassee. Because of her, he is readying himself to stalk streets for supplies her presence alonedeems necessary, streets he just one day ago left two men to die on. So she waits for it, the walk off, the jog, the sprint, whichever speed he'll select for escape. Because Vitri, she knows, owes her nothing else.

Vitri walks to her and crouches. In one hand is a pistol, this one slightly smaller than the one he has in his waistband, and narrower, the same matte black, the grip just as ridged. His mouth moves beneath the scarf as he points at, presses and pulls mechanisms on the pistol, sights to safety to trigger. When he hands it over to her, his eyes shift to the window, then to the floor. He loops his hand as if he is signaling some sort of scheme that Reyn, though she cannot follow, is to play a critical role in. And then, without so much as a nod or wave, Vitri stands, pulls his backpack over his shoulders, and walks out of the room.

Petrified of its weight, Reyn sets the pistol on the floor. She tries to stand but dizzies herself doing so. Her tongue throbs. Her cheek throbs. Her entire head throbs.

She thinks of the skinned knees she never really had, the scraped elbows, the fat lips, thinks of the classmates she'd watch once she turned seven, the odd-shaped balls they'd toss, the discs, how they would fall, and fight, and cry, and bleed. She thinks of their pain, their sudden but short-lived discomfort, and cannot shake the exaggerated image of their rising, of their limp back home, to the park, nursing their arms as they search their phones for the nearest ice cream truck, joyously licking while blood streaks to their wrists. They sprint those scars home and—

ALL WE CAN DO IS GROW WITH THEM

Reyn tries to remember the day her father wrote that. A Saturday or Sunday. She was five, maybe six. He had a moustache then, and shoulder-length hair he'd, per the restaurant's requirements, bundle beneath a hairnet, which lent to the nickname of Honeycomb, as coined by one of his prep cooks. Reyn remembers he'd just woken and was tying around his waist the work apron he hadn't washed for months. And it was there, on that couch she'd so often watch those children from, he'd sat next to her and lit a cigarette. She remembers not being able to take her eyes off of his fingers, filthy as they were, scarred as they were, nicked by various knives over the years. She remembers asking about his scars that day, to which he smiled, and wrote what he wrote. But then he pointed to his left forearm, to a curved pink line from thumb to elbow that looked to Reyn like two strands of yarn braided together and stretched taut. She remembers asking him how it happened.

MY MOM SLEPT WITH ZEKE REY. MY DAD PUNCHED A WINDOW. SO I PUNCHED A WINDOW

After that, he'd lit another cigarette and, instead of waiting around to answer the questions he'd prompted, he'd kissed her head and left for work, returning home with new bandages around his right thumb and forefinger.

Inches from the window now, hung quilt cocooning her shoulders, Reyn opens her mouth as wide as she can. What the window faintly reflects back at her is an engorged tongue with black swirls on the top, side and bottom. Still warm to the touch but ribbed like tree bark. Reyn takes her fingers out of her mouth and crumbles the specks of black grit that have clung to her fingertips. She closes her mouth, twists her neck, inspects her left cheek, then her right. How swollen, how engulfed they are in bright purples and bright yellows. The panic she works to hush doesn't allow her to understand it now, but the bruises will get worse before they get better—the swelling will decrease, and her eyes will once again approach normality; those bright purples and yellows will exhale to violet, will stretch, will deepen.

What pulls her from this hole she's dug fails to bring her absolute relief; rather, it redirects her worry back to what forced her from the floor and carried her to the window: one block to the west, Vitri appears, out of the shadows and into the sunlit street, eyes monitoring east, then west as he walks north, two hands on his pistol, avoiding piles of chipped marble, sidestepping stray shards of glass, breeze swirling debris around his calves. Once he crosses the street, he steps into an alley, out of Reyn's sight.

As she backs away, part of the quilt snags on the windowsill, leaving a gap through which sunlight spills onto the floor. Reyn grabs three severed legs of some table and has every intention of placing them in the fire. But she doesn't see the point. Her face is so very hot. Smoke continues to dry her eyes. They have wood, plenty of wood, enough kindling, and matches; another fire could be started without struggle. So, discarding Vitri's request, Reyn sets the pieces of wood down and continues toward the wall she'd risen from moments ago. Once there, she eases her way to the floor and, for a moment, watches the smoke ascend to the ceiling—faint puffs that evolve into elaborate coils.

Reyn then turns her attention to what Vitri had removed from his backpack and set on the floor: four aluminum cans, three bottles of water, one pair of socks, three almond-scented candles. There is a thin magazine, too, doormatting the water bottles, its front cover face down.

DEEP THROAT

She has seen that phrase before, on gas station magazine stands, and on search engine bars, appearing as a recent option to return to whenever she'd type the D and E of DEAF on her father's keyboard. It does strike her as odd, however, that it is in Vitri's possession, that it is something he carries so close when he carries so little otherwise. Odd, but not uncommon, that he has deemed the brunette beneath the lime green letters beautiful. She sits on a piano bench, her hands masking her large breasts. Her eyes are shut. Red lips parted. Hair and torso damp. Reyn thinks that the woman cannot be older than twenty, then wonders if her mother had looked like that once, legs thick, free of surface vein, tan and smooth, if, before Reyn ruined her, she'd had a stomach just as flat as hers, breasts just as round.

Flipping past advertisements for cannabis and vodka, and several more for cologne and phone hotlines, Reyn finds more photographs of the cover woman, the first being a severe close-up of her breasts, merlot fingernails over her nipples. Its caption: PAINTER WHITE PLAYS WITH HER TITS. The next is of Painter's groin, pink razor in hand, pubic hair as thin as an eyebrow: PAINTER WHITE SHAVES HER PUSSY. Reyn flips the page: Painter White is on her back. Reyn flips: Painter White is upright, staring off camera. Advertisement, advertisement, advertisement. Painter White's arm is reaching for the erect penis that has entered the frame. Reyn flips: Painter White's mouth is open, eyes squinted, gunk stringing across her nose and lashes, off of her chin. PAINTER WHITE GETS PAINTED WHITE.

Reyn flips back to PAINTER WHITE PLAYS WITH HER TITS. She sets the open magazine on the floor, then stands. Careful not to bump her cheek or mouth, Reyn removes her sweatshirt and tosses it aside. The white t-shirt she has worn beneath for months has stretched so loose that if wind were to pass through the room it would flap behind her like a cape. She eases that off, too, and looks down at her breasts, squeezed by the too-small beige training bra her mother had found for her once she'd outgrown the others. She looks down. She looks at the magazine. Compares. Covers her breasts.

Reyn flips to the front cover, then swiftly kicks off her shoes and unbuttons her jeans. She looks at Painter. She looks at herself. At Painter, at herself. Painter, herself. Painter. Clumps of hair do not dwell under Painter's arms, or beneath her waistband. Painter's face is not busted. Stubble does not shade Painter's legs. Painter is not pale and narrow but tan and sculpted, a work of art captured for and desired by men, even

84

men like Vitri, kind men, rescuers, caretakers. *Inferior.* That's what this exercise has confirmed. Reyn is inferior. Subjacent. Baggage left behind instead of something to be sought, if only for moments. The acceptance of this—the way it continues to gnaw its way through her sore gums—eclipses her desire to be Painter White. It inflames her. She wants to rid the world of this woman. Rip her from those pages. Ball her like mountain snow, and toss her into the trashcan. Yet, without an inkling as to why, all Reyn does is gawk, and flip, gawk, and flip. Until the anger is no longer external, until she has embodied it, until she has twisted her way into becoming its incognizant carrier.

Reyn tosses Painter White back to the floor and pulls her jeans to her waist and buttons them. She stomps into her shoes. With little consideration of the pain in her face, she jostles her head through the collar of her white t-shirt. Does the same with her sweatshirt. Untangles her hair. She then walks to her backpack against the wall, crouches, unzips the largest pocket, and plunges her hand in, fingers searching for TIME. She wants to change the conversation she's having with herself. Wants to search the magazines for what is to become her new home, more than what the tourism ads she barely remembers can provide, the blue-green waves, coastal castle, and designer bottle of rum saying very little about San Juan's people. She wants an article. A profile. Something. She wants to know so that, should he return, she can converse with Vitri about San Juan, about the culture they'll be adopting. Wants to appear intelligent about at least one thing. Wants to pull her weight with at least one thing. More importantly, she wants to feel excited once more, not primed for abandonment, not shamed by filthy pictures of a beautiful woman. But her hands find nothing but food cans. Plastic bottles she nudges aside. The cold metal of a small, adjustable wrench at the bottom.

Confused, Reyn extracts her hand. She looks around the room as if somewhere in its emptiness the magazines have been tucked. She turns toward the quilt-covered windows. Through the gap she'd unintentionally left, the sky is graying by the second, scurrying to black. The quilt quivers. She can feel in her feet a dull vibration transmitting through the hardwood floor. Tremors that tell her to stand. And that's all she does. She does not back away. She does not walk to that window. She stands, and she thinks: *We've been tracked.* She pictures a cluster of masked men and women—red, yellow, both—standing on the street, weapons ready, the darkness an illusion, a diversion for the rabid few sprinting the staircase. It's a thought that motivates her to sprint across the room and shut the door. She searches for a lock—finds none. She grabs the trashcan with the intention of swiveling it in front of the door—it's too hot for her hands. So Reyn grabs the pistol. She backs away while her hands find its grip, and once ready, she stops. Takes aim at the door.

Ten seconds pass. Her outstretched arm trembles. Thirty. *You can do this*, she thinks. *You are capable.* Another ten seconds, another thirty. Nothing. The door handle hasn't been turned. She crouches and places her free hand on the floor, feeling for sprints, for stomps, though little can be distinguished over the tremors from the other side of the window. Either nothing is beneath her, or everything, more of the masked than she'd initially assumed, more than just a cluster. Eight of them, she thinks, ten of them, twelve.

Reyn waits another thirty seconds. Nothing. The tremors outside lessen, but only slightly. She stands. Lets her outstretched arm ease to her side. Turns to the window. She sees that it's lighter now. Lighter, and lighter, and lighter, darkness from before peeling back like a scab. She squeezes once more between the quilt and the windows. A fist-sized crack is now in the upper right corner, its thin veins stretching toward the sill. The grey cloud before the building shrinks, from fifteen-feet wide to twelve, to ten, narrowing itself back into a manhole on the street below, fifty yards or so from where Vitri had crossed. Bits of brick and marble rain on the street. Thumb-sized shreds of wood. Paper floats about.

Miles north, another grey cloud takes shape. Up it rises, up-up-up like stairs, higher than the tallest building, then higher yet, and wider, as if there are arms within to be spread, a black hug to offer the sky. Then, another rises, miles east. Another, west.

Reyn looks back to the manhole on the street below, half-expecting to see Vitri emerge. She wonders if he is the orchestrator of this. Wonders if her panic was pointless, is pointless. Wonders if this is what he spoke of from behind that scarf, the language of his hand: "Blacken the city, escape with darkness." But, with the immediate cloud completely retracted, it becomes clear that there's no movement near or within that manhole, from Vitri or otherwise.

Two hundred yards north, however, a motorcycle skids from an alley, across the street, and into a lamppost. At the sight, Reyn crouches beneath the windowsill. Seconds later she raises her curious eyes to see the motorcycle's yellow-masked driver stumbling in the street, dazed, searching for his balance. He falls. He pushes himself back to his feet. Falls down again. He keeps looking behind him and, after he falls once more, Reyn understands why: sprinting from the same alley are two red-masked men.

Navy blue briefcase in hand, Vitri sprints across the street, away from the crash, and down the alley leading to the furniture store. He'd watched it unravel from from streets over, through an abandoned art gallery's fogged windows: the motorcycle, the crash, the stumble. He'd glimpsed the masked. And he'd at first hurried south. Away from Reyn. *To Tallahassee alone*, like he'd intended, leaving her with more than anyone would give him: food, fire, a loaded pistol, the hope that he'd come back for her, the façade that, yes, there may still be wanderers capable of humanity, to go out of their way to save, out of their way to heal. And so he'd guiltlessly jogged south, his pack light, one balled raincoat in his hand, 9mm in his right.

What turned him around—what spurred him back to that clothing store, to that second raincoat, to that navy blue briefcase, and now back here, to feeding briefcase and backpack through the one furniture store window he'd broken yesterday and scraped clean with this very pistol barrel—was the fact that Reyn had watched him sign his birth name to a lie. He pictured her tucking those words into a pocket, studying the exchange for days, too naïve, too optimistic to burn the pages, to set the damn notebook down and leave, just leave, emerging from the furniture store only in search of him, rather than restarting her initial path to nowhere.

She isn't your responsibility. You shouldn't care what happens to her. But he does. He absolutely does. Because they do. His audience, it's back—his boy, his wife, swimming in his fragile conscious, warning of the guilt he'd shoulder if he left Reyn alone in this inconceivable place.

After Vitri vaults himself over the windowsill, he hustles to the nearest staircase. Up he goes, up-up-up, to the second floor door. He opens the door into the hallway and slows his pace so as not to spook Reyn. Wood smoke swirls into the hall from beneath the closed door. Vitri approaches, presses his ear to the door. No footsteps. The popping of plastic by flame.

"Reyn, it's me," Vitri says from behind the scarf, now blotted grey by the soot still descending outside. "Reyn?"

Vitri opens the door slowly. Feet from the door is the trashcan and, beyond that, at the window and staring north, somewhere between crouching and standing, is Reyn, torso half-wrapped in the quilt. Without shutting the door, Vitri steps around the trashcan and into the room.

"Hey," he says. "Don't watch that."

Reyn shifts her weight but, still, she doesn't respond. She doesn't turn around.

Vitri steps closer. "It's okay, Reyn." He tosses the briefcase on the floor.

A gunshot rings out.

Vitri covers his throbbing ears.

Reyn turns around, pistol in hand.

"Are you fucking deaf?" He watches Reyn step out of the quilt, toward him, revealing a single bullet hole in the window. Vitri's stomach tilts. His ears are still adjusting. "Fuck, fuck, fuck," he says, striding to the window. Three-hundred yards out, one red-masked man forces the rider's intestine over a parking meter, a struggle halted only when he is waved forward by his counterpart, who on his own has advanced toward the furniture store.

Vitri turns, grabs Reyn by the shoulders, and says, "We need to get out of here." Tears are in her eyes. The .22 pistol is no longer in her hand. "We need to get out of here," Vitri repeats. He crouches, picks up the pistol. Places it in his waistband. "Do you hear me?"

Reyn doesn't move. Can barely look at him. Stares at the window instead. Wipes her eyes. She, Vitri understands now, can't hear him. She hasn't heard him, not now, not last night. She hasn't heard a single word that he's said.

He shuts his eyes. *South, south, south.*

Still crouched, Vitri reaches for the pen they'd left on the hardwood floor and, after standing, shoves it in his front pocket. He then nudges Reyn forward, around the trashcan, to the hallway and toward the staircase. He makes her walk in front and up they go, toward the third floor, the sound of their creaking steps yawning along the walls, overpowered only by the sound of masked shoulders ramming the ground level door, the sound of the furniture Vitri had turned into obstacles skidding across the concrete.

"Go, go, go," Vitri says to Reyn. They pass the door to the third floor's hallway.

A loud thud from below. A desk or dresser toppling over.

"Fucking go," Vitri says. As if she were a horse, he swats at Reyn's right hip with an open hand. Again and again, and off she goes, up the staircase, to the fourth floor, until more than a few feet are between she and Vitri. Halfway up the staircase, due to what Vitri suspects is an uneven equilibrium, Reyn slips, falls, her left knee crashing into one particular step with enough force for the old wood to bow beneath her weight. Within seconds, she is back on her feet and continuing up the staircase.

Thud below, skid below, more furniture being displaced, a path being cleared.

Vitri leaps over the bowed step and reaches the top. This door, as he'd discovered the night before, doesn't open to a hallway, but to a large, carpeted room with fifteen-foot ceilings, overcast sky protruding through the two windows on the west wall, through the hatched skylight above. Blotches of faded pink paint linger on the walls. There is a nook at the south end of the room housing two vending machines, each with gaping holes crowbarred above their deposit doors, coils of stripped wire spilling out. And there are three tipped café tables—two in the center of the room and one tucked near that nook, in the southeast corner.

After easing the door shut, Vitri grabs Reyn's arm and leads her to one of the café tables in the center of the room. He points at the carpet behind the table—GET

DOWN. Reyn, without hesitation, drops to her knees and inches toward the table's metal legs, body partially hidden by the tipped surface of the table. Once she settles, Vitri widens his palm—STAY. Reyn nods. Vitri pulls the pen from his pocket and crouches. Rolls up her sweatshirt sleeve and frantically writes on her left forearm.

1 LET THEM WALK IN
2 THEY'LL WALK TO YOU
3 DON'T LOOK AT ME
4 I'LL SHOOT
5 IF I DIE YOU'LL SHOOT

As Reyn reads, Vitri pulls the .22 pistol from his waistband. He isn't going to hand it over until she nods, until she acknowledges that here, in the center of this room, she is to be bait. After she does nod, Vitri hands the pistol over, then quietly flips the café table nearest to the door upside down, onto its surface, and slides it across the carpet to the northeast corner of the room. He kneels behind the table, pistol barrel steadied on the narrow bar connecting leg to leg.

Over his breath he can hear them—somewhere below, he can hear them. Second floor, third floor, something is rolling across the hardwood. Slowly, achingly so. Then, a door handle. A door latching. Vitri looks at Reyn, whose exhalations are seesawing his, and holds his index finger to his scarved lips. Presses his ear to the north wall.

Creeaak—

—creeeeeaaaaak-creak-creak-creeeeeaaaaak—

—creaks from one pair of feet, then two—

—creak-creeeaaak-creak-creeeaaak—

—the sound slows, then trails, as if they, convinced that their ears and eyes had played tricks on them, had turned around on the staircase, had given up and were ready to settle for the rider they'd mutilated. And soon there is no sound beyond that door. Nothing at all. Vitri looks to Reyn. Other than gingerly wiping sweat from her bruised cheek, she is still. She is calm. Eyes on the door, braced for whatever may barge through—

—SNAP—

—*Reyn's knee*, Vitri thinks, the step she bowed now split in two—

—creak-creak-creak-creak, creak-creak-creak-creak—

Vitri waves his left hand until Reyn looks his way. When he has Reyn's attention he points to his scarf as if it were a mask, then to the door. She nods. Looks briefly at her inked arm before returning her eyes to the door. Vitri grips the 9mm. Tighter now. Tighter.

The doorknob turns.

Vitri glances at Reyn. IF I MISS, he wishes he'd written, knowing that failure here will be far worse for her. Yanked by the hair. Dragged. Raped. KILL YOURSELF.

The door opens.

The tip of the point man's Bowie knife is the first thing that Vitri sees. It creeps, it lurks, it hovers, it grows, it shimmers as the point man cranes his neck to assess what's beyond the doorway. And then Reyn is spotted. Vitri can see it in her eyes—strained, scared, wanting to flee but consciously denying the desire.

The door opens further.

A faded brown boot comes into view. A shin, a thigh, a waist, a bicep. The Bowie knife is twirled. Shoulders bob forward as if sea. Neck, head. One step, two steps, three steps, four—

Vitri fires.

To the floor drops the point man, to the air once more goes Vitri's hearing, to the vending machine crawls Reyn, and through the doorway hurries the second masked man, turning, turning, stomping directly toward Vitri, a sickle secure in his right hand.

Vitri fires.

The masked man drops the sickle and clutches his gushing throat. Yet he continues toward Vitri, stomping until the stomps slow to toe drags. Eight feet and closing, stomping, staggering, stomping, dragging, bleeding all over himself.

Vitri stands. He waits for the masked man to come closer. Just a bit closer. Five feet, three feet. Aims. Fires. Down goes the man's hands, buckled are his knees.

Vitri looks to the point man, who, though injured, continues to dig his fingernails into the carpet and slither himself after Reyn. Reyn, pistol still in hand, has nearly backed up to the nook now. Vitri steps over his tipped café table and hustles to the point man.

He steps on the man's back; can feel his groan transmitted to his toes. Presses the barrel of the 9mm to the back of his head. Pulls the trigger.

Vitri looks at Reyn, who, backed all the way to the nook now, won't take her eyes from the body Vitri stands upon. She is crying.

"Why are you crying?" Vitri says, feeling his way through the question rather than hearing it. "Huh? Why the fuck are you crying?" He walks toward her now, scarf shifting with his lips, feet gaining momentum as she cowers. His hearing is coming back. "Four people I've killed because of you. Four fucking people." Vitri snatches the pistol from Reyn's hand.

Vitri stands to the side of the second-floor window, peeking beneath the quilt. A dark green plane circles overhead. Straightens its path; descends slightly. Out of its cargo bay falls a black rectangle, small when compared to the tan parachute that unfolds seconds after to slow the plummet. Vitri watches the wind take the supply block north. Watches three red-masked men emerge from the manhole below and chase after it on foot, around vehicles, through alleys.

The plane flies east, toward the last of a dark grey cloud. Circles, straightens, descends, unloads another rectangle. It isn't until moments later, after the three red-masked men have returned and are assembly-lining black duffel bags down the manhole, that Vitri turns around and communicates to Reyn that they'll leave in the middle of night.

BORN DEAF?
YEAH
SIGN LANGUAGE?
SOME. I READ. I WRITE
YOU'RE GOOD AT IT
CAN WE TALK ABOUT SOMETHING ELSE?
SURE
WHERE ARE MY MAGAZINES?
FIRE
SYRINGES?
FIRE
WHY?
YOURS?
MOTHER'S.
DRUG?

```
                    OHAPILA. MASKED MAKE IT
                            WHO?
        EAST OF HERE. BY MONROE. MASKS. YELLOW
              YELLOW IS FROM MONROE?
                 I THINK SO. LOTS OF THEM
                    SHOULDN'T GO EAST?
                            NO
                      WHAT'S SOUTH?
                      I DON'T KNOW
                  WE'LL GO SOUTH THEN
                            OK
                 WE'LL FOLLOW THE COAST
                            OK
                    SOMETHING WRONG?
                 WHAT'S IN THE BRIEFCASE?
                       RAINCOATS
                 HASN'T RAINED IN A WHILE
           WAS TOLD THERE ARE CHEMICAL RAINS
                            OK
        WHY DO YOU KEEP LOOKING AT THE CEILING?
             UP THERE, WHAT DID YOU SAY TO ME?
                      I WAS ANGRY
                        I KNOW
           I DIDN'T SAY ANYTHING IMPORTANT
                    THOSE TWO MEN?
                  WHAT ABOUT THEM?
                       NOTHING
                  WHAT ABOUT THEM?
             CAN WE LOOK AT THEIR FACES?
```

###

The room smells of excrement, that which had been abandoned by each of these bodies still finding ways to surface. Grimacing through the stench, Reyn and Vitri roll the trailer over first. Various scars cover his shaved head, some the width of a fingernail, some more as long as a soda can, and others that seem to have been inflicted by the hands of another. There's modification of seeming intention as well though, multiple crescents marching in pairs above the neck and along the crown, like moons to a warped parade deck. Off-ruby stones on fishhooks droop from each earlobe. His neck has been stained so heavily that an entry wound cannot be located. Where there aren't bloodstains, it appears as if his skin hadn't only been shielded from the sun for stretches at a time, but that for months it had been scrubbed with some bleaching agent. Veiny, bloated. Since his death, his red vest has compressed to his chest, tight enough that the center button's stitching has begun to unwind. Beneath, on his gut, Reyn sees a tattooed red hand— much too small to be his hand. The hand of a woman, she believes. jagged along the fingernails, made illegible by the soaked and matted chest hair.

93

Vitri tosses the sickle toward the door, then waves for Reyn to hover the candle over the trailer's face. Leaning in, Reyn sees that there is a small bullet hole in the man's leather mask, above his right eyebrow. There are eye fissures, tear-shaped holes for nostrils, a mouth-hole wide enough to feed a small spoon through. Along the jaw and hairline, the mask is sewn to the trailer's face, stitches an inch apart at most but, as if they'd run out of thread, from right ear to chin the mask is anchored to flesh by construction staples. Vitri places his scarf on the carpet and looks at Reyn. She shrugs her shoulders. He grabs the notebook, writes.

STILL WANT TO?

Reyn nods. She wants to. She needs to. Needs to see who these people are. Believes that by doing so, some form of clarity can be had. History. Purpose. Theirs. Hers. Why they are here, dead. Why she and Vitri are alive, why she's still in Louisiana, why she has yet to put on a mask, things she's never thought could be answered by staring at a stranger's face. She expects Vitri to feel the same way, but all he does is stare at her, then at the man, his eyes sadly alert, his bottom lip between his teeth. WE SHOULDN'T DO THIS, the stare says. Reyn sets the candle down and asks for the notebook.

I'LL DO IT

Vitri shakes his head. He pulls his knife from a pants pocket. Points at the candle and, once Reyn again brings the flame over the man's face, starts in on the staples, digging the point of the blade into the man's flesh, then prying the staple's center. At first, the trailer's skin resists. Lifts with the knife. Shivers with the knife. Descends with the knife. Won't let go. Vitri twists the blade, lays it flat, applies his weight to the handle for seconds. Then, pluck, out it comes, bloodless, still bent around the loose bit of leather. Reyn, despite her curiosity, can only focus on Vitri's right hand, on the wounds she'd given him the night before. Teethmarks from knuckle to knuckle, dried blood black in the dim light. I DON'T WANT THIS TO HURT YOU, Reyn considers writing, I'M SORRY.

Having established an effective method—dig, twist, pluck—Vitri quickly makes his way through the staples. Reyn takes it upon herself to lift what Vitri has freed of the mask. She peeks beneath; glimpses long, tangled hairs. Grey roots, black centers, red tips. And then Vitri grabs her hand. Removes it from the mask, redirects the candlelight over the man's forehead, and dives back in, slicing through four of the stitches. He cuts through more—two, three—then slides his hand beneath the loose half of the mask. Grips tight. And rips. Three more stitches out. He angrily resets the trailer's tilting head, and rips. Two more. Reset, rip, until the mask is off.

There is bruising around the entry wound. Swelling, too, as far down as the trailer's eye, reducing the oval to a slit. The other eye is open, wide open, whites strained red, the center a light purple. It is all Vitri needs to see. Knife in hand, he stands and walks to the point man across the room. But Reyn stays. Examines the man further. A nose whose hook has been intensified by the mask. Parched lips at a diagonal. Faint crow's feet looping each eye. He is no younger than forty-five, and reminds her of no one.

Which makes it difficult for Reyn to decipher the feeling she has when looking at the dead man. It isn't pity. It isn't sorrow. And it isn't satisfaction. She studies him for as long as she can, before it dawns on her that Vitri is without direct light. But it isn't enough time for her speculation to mesh itself into anything cohesive, anything detailed regarding this dead man's life. She pictures a faceless woman. A fast car, something he'd tinker with. Pictures a gentle dog by his side. No, a cat. He looks more like a cat person. *Ralph*, she thinks. She's never known a Ralph. Has no basis for this. *You look like a Ralph.* And it is only in this way that Reyn feels closer to him, understanding of him, his life, its motives, how what she believes had to have been positive experiences go ignored, are trumped instead by an irreversible pull towards the power that comes with no longer caring whether or not your actions are for good. That freedom found by her mother, by her father.

Before she crosses the room, Reyn drapes Vitri's scarf over her arm and grabs the notebook with her free hand. She turns and, if he weren't leaned against the bit of wall directly beneath the window, moonlight on his scalp, Reyn wouldn't be able to see Vitri. Puzzled, she walks to the point man, candlelight flickering with each step—he lies on his back, mask off, face up, Vitri's knife across his neck. His nose has been flattened.

His lips are parched. He has the same earrings as Ralph, the same tattoo. There is matted facial hair, but it is blonde, wispy, young. The eyes are young. The cheeks are young. The point man is a boy, a tall, lanky boy with a swimmer's torso, lump left half-developed in his throat.

Reyn looks at Vitri. He stares at the floor but keeps pressing his hands together, fingers waging war with one another, grappling for something, anything. Reyn wonders if Vitri had known the boy in a previous life. Nephew, neighbor, employee, some title that now reminds him of just what his heart is for. When Vitri finally looks up at Reyn, it is with wet eyes. Tragic eyes, eyes of anger, eyes of regret, eyes of grief, and—she can place the look—Vitri is lost, utterly lost.

Reyn drops the notebook, carefully sets the candle nearby, then crouches in front of Vitri. As he lowers his head, Reyn follows with her hand and dabs his wet face with the scarf. She watches his still-grappling fingers.

Eventually Vitri grabs her, not with malice, but with enough strength to tug her toward him, close, within his arms, to his chest. He holds her tight, so tight, so very tight, and his hands move all over—from back to neck, from neck to shoulders, from shoulders to arms, massaging, scratching, shifting, stroking her hair. Calming those fingers. Vitri then kisses Reyn on the top of her head. He kisses her near the temple. He kisses her on the cheek. Again. And again.

Vitri is flying—no, no, he isn't flying, but he isn't walking, isn't jumping, isn't running; he is seated but still soaring through the sky—ascending, knifing through clouds. He is atop something, some soundless creature he, because he can feel its power as it flaps its wings. He lets his arms dangle, lets his fingers wander the creature's dry skin—there are no feathers; scales; stubble. He swivels his head. Tries to see through the clouds, through the dense fog below. It troubles him that there is no scent on the air. Only a sound, a hummed melody, a

doo-doo-daahhh-dah-doo-doo-daahhh-dah,

and as much as he strains to listen, as much as he strains to see, there is nothing, no source,

doo-doo-daahhh-dah-doo-doo-daahhh-dah,

doo-doo-daahhh-dah-doo-doo-daahhh-dah,

a woman's voice, a raspy voice, a weakening voice, siphoned from the sky, plummeting to what lies beneath, vaulting him toward panic, to reach, to itch, to gasp. And then the creature is no more, and he is falling. Falling after the voice, falling, falling, falling straight down, slow at first but accelerating through the fog, into darkness, until he, without so much as a surface ripple, is underwater, on his back, staring at a refracted moon, bloated, bright, and chambered in by swinging bands of stars. When he tries to roll himself into swimming position, he's shoved further beneath the surface—one meter, two meters, three, that panic returning in the form of a scream, voice distorted by the water, by the soaked scarf that has untied itself, and is now stretched over his face, yanking him

doo-doo-daahhh-dah-doo-doo-daahhh-dah,

deeper now, a voice he has never heard,

doo-doo-daahhh-dah-doo-doo-daahhh-dah,

and over him floats a rusted tricycle with white handlebars, over him floats a crumpled flashcard, over him floats his son, his grey feet, his grey legs—snug in his pinstriped pajama bottoms—then his grey torso, his grey, water-shriveled face. Blood seeps from the his son's ears and spins counter-clockwise, strands of red dissipating with the wake Vitri creates with his clawing hands. But then his son is gone, past, and Vitri keeps

97

moving, because he cannot stop, and he keeps on clawing, he keeps on reaching, because it's the only thing he knows how to do. And then, like that, his hands are granted control of the moon, of the stars, and, before he is aware of the power he wields, he wrenches them into the water, until he is shrouded in white light,

doo-doo-daahhh-dah-doo-doo-daahhh-dah,

and over him floats an upside down frying pan, over him floats a pair of black flats, a yellow sundress, over him are suds, lilac-scented suds funneling toward him as if he were a drain sending the sea to land, lilac-scented suds outlining ten toes, dripping from a woman's smooth calves, a woman's thin thighs,

doo-doo-daahhh-dah-doo-doo-daahhh-dah,

and he stops reaching, stops clawing, stops moving altogether. Gives up. And then he is lifted. Toward the surface, toward the moon and the stairs, toward the woman, her groin, her torso, her breasts, her neck—

From the metal trashcan, Reyn watches Vitri's hand twitch. Asleep, he looks so much like a child, so serene, so at ease. Adorable. Legs curled, cuddled against the west wall, drooling on the cap end of his water bottle pillow, his body a respiring mound in the far reaches of the candle's glow. She feels as if she could watch him like this for hours.

Leaving the lit candle by the trashcan, Reyn tiptoes to the door, where she has set the briefcase and their zipped backpacks. She hopes that Vitri will appreciate that upon awakening, her effort, how much time she has saved by packing for the both of them. She wants him to nod, to smile. To wrap his arms around her like before and squeeze, and hold, and hold, and hold. For now, though, she's in search of something. She unzips the largest pocket of Vitri's backpack and, in doing so, causes Vitri to stir. She extracts an unlit candle only when he has settled, then, careful of the noise, she slowly unzips her own backpack and wrests out Ralph's sickle. Items in hand, she returns to the trashcan. Sits cross-legged on the floor, facing Vitri, the only man other than her father that has ever kissed her.

She knows how childish it is to think anything of it. The man was scared. The man was angry. The man was lost. And Reyn was just the person that happened to be there. Nothing more than within reach. A band-aid. That's all. No man dreams of band-aids, of anything to mend a wound they'd never admit to having. Hours from now—when they are to walk south in silence—days, even, she knows he'll do everything he can to rid his mind of the fourth floor, her included, her especially; Reyn, whose disability set the whole thing in motion.

Feeling so certain of such makes it no easier for Reyn to accept that, for the hours he has been asleep, all she has wanted to do is reciprocate. Kiss him on the forehead. On each cheek. Moments ago, she even lowered herself enough for her breath to move his hair, so close that she could smell the dried tomato soup on his moustache. What stopped her, what brought her here, behind the garbage can, had been anxiety. Her stomach had spun. Her pulse had risen. Her mind had darted to an image of Vitri waking, of Vitri reaching up, of Vitri choking her. She pictured Vitri, so embarrassed, so ashamed, so clueless as to how to interact with her, letting go of his hold, prepping her for what she would assume was their trek to Florida, and then trading her to the masked. For a weapon. For a vehicle. For a masked Painter White, a specialist in the field of wounds.

Reyn straightens the unlit candle's crooked wick, then tilts it to the flame of its lit counterpart. Once the new candle holds the flame, she sets it on the floor. Brings the old candle close. Examines the layer of melted wax atop, the black burn marks across the glass, the smudges and slashes—high, low, thick, thin, jagged, rounded. Before blowing out the flame, Reyn hovers her nose over the candle's rim and takes one deep breath. *Almonds.* She can't remember ever smelling anything so warm, so welcoming. She imagines them in a small house, one burning on a coffee table during game night, another on a nightstand overlooking a set of ruffled covers. *Pillars*, she thinks. *A home. That's what these are.*

As the wax hardens, Reyn, not unlike the man that machete-slit her tongue, grips the back of Ralph's sickle, clambers her fingers up-up-up until only an inch or two of the blade is visible, dried blood flaking onto her fingers. She then eases the blade into the wax, carving:

R + V

After setting her work on the floor, Reyn peels the clotted wax from the tip of Ralph's sickle, balls it with her fingers and places it in the shallow pool of wax forming in the other candle. She then rises and tiptoes to her backpack. Into the large pocket, behind the pistol Vitri has insisted she carry, goes the sickle. She stuffs R+V between the pages of DEEP THROAT, but not before shoving it into a stray wool sock. There it will cool, and harden, and, she hopes, endure. Because, even if Vitri decides that he wants to forget all of this, she wants to remember what happened here. This man saved her. He healed her. He protected her. Kissed her. Forcing these facts to vanish, she feels, would be tragic.

Reyn zips the pockets of each backpack. Turns to see a water bottle rolling across the floor. Vitri is awake, sitting up, eyes wide and searching, uncertain of his surroundings but becoming acclimated once more. Reyn, carrying a pen and the notebook, walks toward Vitri. But Vitri jumps to his feet. He hurries to the window and yanks the quilt aside. Darkness is lifting, an early morning indigo slipping into its place, the tops of buildings transitioning out of shadow. Vitri lets the quilt swing shut, turns around, stares at Reyn, then raises his arms in question. But all she can focus on is his crotch, on his erection, the bulge of the denim.

I WAS JUST GOING TO WAKE YOU UP
I TOLD YOU NOT TO LET ME SLEEP
YOU NEEDED IT

Reyn stands behind Vitri as he crouches and examines his backpack. She waits for him to turn before presenting the notebook to him. But he ignores her. Looks past her, around her, scanning for something else to cram, anything she may have forgotten. When he finally notices the notebook, Vitri takes it from her. He jams it into her backpack, zips the large pocket shut, then asks for the pen. Once in his hand, Vitri stands. He grabs Reyn's arm, rolls up the sleeve of her sweatshirt and crosses out the instructions from before. Writes:

USE YOUR EYES
STICK TO SHADOWS
HOLD MY HAND

###

Heaps of dead birds on Cotton St. Bent beaks, twisted beaks, cracked beaks, red, blue, and black feathers static, plugged into the damp, dank air. There is a dog, too, dozens of feet away, some mutt with one ear batting its weak paws at a plastic bag dancing in front of a ravaged insurance building. Other than that, in the hours that they've been on foot, it has seemed to Vitri that the streets of Shreveport belong to he and Reyn, and the cars—cars, cars, cars, tires gone, windows smashed, hoods off, guts out—the crumbling of wood and brick chips beneath their feet one of only a few sounds to be heard.

Wary, Vitri quickens their pace. Tugs Reyn's right hand with him through a portion of Loyola's campus, adjusting his focus as the sun does, from roofs and windows to sidewalks and intersections, scanning, searching. They move like this through cemeteries and city parks, past medical centers, past museums, past hotels and libraries, past it all and out of the city.

QUERBES PARK

Vitri leans on the sign. His clothes are heavy with sweat. His feet ache. Though on the air is a scent of vomit, and the garbage cans tipped, the park is rather robust. Fences are intact. Save for white blotches on their tops the size and shape of watermelons, hedges have remained green. Tree branches are bare, soggy leaves now carpeting the yellow grass, the concrete path winding through the park—dark yellow leaves, bright red leaves, see-through mint green. Vitri watches Reyn reach for one from the ground. He grabs her arm.

"Chemicals," he says, then slides the scarf off of his nose. He puts his hands on his hips and scans the area, paying particular attention to a dry water fountain in the center of the park. "Think we're safe?"

101

He turns to see her unzipping her backpack. Hair falls into her eyes. She brushes it away, careful not to bump her cheek. The swelling, Vitri assumes, is at its peak. In one day, maybe two, it will begin its slog back to normalcy, dark purple center gone, yellow edges dissolving. It hasn't slowed her though, as he anticipated it would. Not one bit. She has been step for step with him the entire way, gripping his hand with more strength than he imagined her possessing. And, though her breathing still is somewhat labored, Vitri, having been caught staring at her, spots excitement in her eyes. For being on the move. For being here, in this park. For being here with him.

The girl, Vitri knows, either due to age or to her disability, does not yet know how to conceal her feelings. Resist them. Shove them down. Concentrate them into curling toes. IS NOT THE TIME, he wants to write. HERE IS NOT THE PLACE. But he feels it, in stares such as this, in how sweaty her shy hand had been on the second floor, before dawn, before they descended the staircase. He can even see it in her handwriting now, as she sets the notebook on the surface of the park sign, how, when compared to the first sentences she wrote for him—their rigidity, their lack of both care and strength— she grips the pen as if it were her brush and the letters her paint. So focused. So round, so perfect.

Vitri sighs. Sees no point in it. Doesn't know her age, but knows that, if not young by birth, young at heart. Has never loved. May never find love, not in a world like this, not in a man like him. But he also sees no point in turning the poor girl's only means of communication into ash, not while she is smiling wide enough that he can see the layers of black on her tongue. Suffering comes to Vitri's mind. *Misery. Agony.* Words she understands, words she knows how to spell, but whose true meanings are lost on a girl that has experienced nothing else.

THINK WE'RE SAFE?

Vitri takes the notebook. Looks at Reyn. Nods, then takes off his backpack and pulls from it a bottle of water. He offers it to Reyn.

She sips.

He sips.

Their breathing slows.

Vitri looks across the park. Feels Reyn's gaze upon him. *Just get this deaf girl somewhere safe*, he thinks. *Leave her where she can't hurt herself.* He slides the scarf back over his nose, then walks south, not bothering to offer a hand.

They come upon NEBEKE'S, an auto dealer just off of what Vitri confirms to be the corner of Southfield and Anniston. Behind the half-filled lot is a twenty-foot high mound of dirt that appears as if, perhaps for some sort of renovation, it had been intentionally placed and shaped by machine. Before walking to it, Vitri tries to signal Reyn, first with the wave of one hand, then with the flailing of both arms. But on she goes, oblivious to him, toward the south end of the car lot. And up the mound he walks, heels digging into the dirt, lungs labored.

Atop the mound, Vitri's scarf twitches in the wind. That same scent of vomit is on the air, stronger now that he is higher, the roofs of nearby buildings rotted and appearing as if one footstep from one emaciated man would turn the block to rubble. He is surprised to see as far as he can. Four miles east, likely more. Surprised but pleased at what he sees: beyond sequential mounds of dirt like the one he stands upon is a large bridge arching over what he knows to be the Red River, sunlight glaring off its skeleton. The river itself, from this distance, looks nothing like a river at all, but a crater. A direct drop off from the east and west banks. Motionless sludge at the bottom. He focuses once more on the bridge. Pictures wooden bridges further south, their footboards snapped, carried by water or by hand to the gulf. Pictures himself trudging through the bottom of the river, backpack held above his head. Pictures cornering himself into the improvisation of some sort of raft for Reyn. Pictures himself drowning in the mud, and her, stuck at sea. *We cross now*, he thinks. *We go east.*

He looks down on the lot. Nearest to the street is a row of wounded hybrids that, like the subsequent rows of sedans and SUVs, extend two hundred feet south. He hadn't noticed it before; couldn't have from the ground—each vehicle's roof has been marked with one red M, painted by both can and brush.

Vitri pulls the 9mm from his waistband and stumbles down the mound, making his way to the middle row once on concrete, searching for Reyn through cracked windshields. Halves of hoods have been sawn off, batteries lifted entirely, pistons and gaskets strewn about, leftover, discarded. The engine of a Sonata is missing, the air filter of an Elantra. And still, no Reyn. Vitri drops to the pavement and looks beneath each sedan. Then, each hybrid, all four tires of every other gone, rolled away. Nothing else. Oil stains. Washers.

Then there is the sound of a dreary car horn. Again.

Vitri stands.

Again.

He scans the lot for the sound. Aims his pistol at nothing in particular.

Another honk, this one quieter, lighter.

Vitri rotates his body toward the sound, toward the back row, the southeast corner of the lot. There, in the driver's seat of a dented silver Jeep sits Reyn, one hand on the wheel, the other dangling out of the shattered driver's side window. She waves at Vitri. Even has the audacity to smile.

She was trying to be quiet, Vitri tells himself as he jogs to the Jeep. He pictures two or three red-masked men sprinting from across the street and into the lot, searching for the origin of such noise. *She was trying to be quiet, she was trying to be quiet, she was trying to be quiet.*

By the time he reaches the Jeep, Reyn has leaned over and opened the passenger door for him. At first he refuses to get in. Makes a waving motion with the pistol instead that he assumes Reyn will take to mean, WE NEED TO LEAVE. The thought, however, never seems to cross her mind. When she isn't waving him in, Reyn is pointing at the dashboard.

Vitri surrenders. He quietly shuts the door after climbing onto the passenger's seat. Once in, he looks all around the Jeep, at the critter-clawed back seat, at the dirt-caked floor, in the glove compartment, the only artifact in the vehicle being its manual. Then he stares as wickedly at Reyn as he can, for as long as he can, a look he hopes will communicate what he feels: YOU'RE FUCKING THIS UP. But the girl isn't to be broken. She smiles. She points again at the dashboard.

I LIVED IN A JEEP WITH MY MOTHER FOR A YEAR
WHY?
NOWHERE ELSE TO GO
LOTS OF PLACES TO GO
MOM DIDN'T THINK SO
WHAT DID YOU DO FOR A YEAR?
SEARCHED. FOR FOOD. WATER, GAS, SYRINGES. READ
DRIVE US OUT OF HERE?
I COULD
ALWAYS WANTED TO TEACH
NEVER HAVE?
NO
KIDS?
COMPLICATED

Way east are engines, loud engines, gas engines, small engines, roaring engines, high-pitched, piercing. Louder now, higher now, louder, higher, nearing NEBEKE'S. Vitri palms Reyn's head and presses it down, until she, taking the hint, balls herself beneath the dash, ankles hooked around the pedals. Then he too tucks himself, as far as a grown man can, chin between the glove compartment and seat. He looks at Reyn as she, beneath the steering wheel, somehow turns herself around, eyes now inches from the driver's seat. Vitri holds his finger to his mouth. QUIET.

The engines are closer now, louder. Vitri counts three of them, distinct if he strains his ears, the lead engine sounding like a cross between a moped and a helicopter, high but snarling when slowing or cornering. The second thumps low like a chopper, one twist of the throttle sounding as if it were grinding asphalt, arcing it behind the vehicle like a waverunner would water. Vitri looks at Reyn, who has shoved her arm beneath the seat. Her arm wiggles; metal clangs. Vitri grips her arm. Points at his scarved face, then to the window—MASKED OUTSIDE—and it seems to be enough to scare her still.

While the sound of the first two engines fade, one lingers, and it hardly sounds like an engine at all to Vitri. Mystical almost, as if it gracefully hovers over a force primed to explode. He imagines three industrial-sized magnets spaced just feet apart.

"Why we stoppin'?" A boy's voice, a pubescent voice, cracking over the sound.

A woman's voice: "How the fuck you expect to drag those reds out them holes from here, Crow?"

"We need some juice." Gruff but somehow neutral, patient. "D'you rather be sittin' duck in the city?"

The woman, rasp fading: "I'm gonna cut that dick off later if I find out you're just pissin'. Old as shit man, swear I'll cut that dick off." There are three loud clangs then, scrapes, the sound of metal being severed. Twenty feet from the Jeep, thirty at most.

The boy: "Hurry up, Crow."

Vitri waits for the scraping to stop, then peeks over the Jeep's dash. Through several windows appears a distorted Crow, elbow deep under the hood of a chardonnay-toned hybrid. He is a shirtless black man in torn off-white pants and, when he lifts the battery from the car, Vitri can see a yellow mask on his face—a hockey goalie's mask, with a jagged hole cut around the mouth. Vitri dips his head when Crow turns toward the Jeep. Reyn attempts to rise and, again, Vitri palms her head. Forces her still. Forces her quiet.

When he peeks over the dash again, Crow is walking north, between the hybrids and sedans, toward the woman and the boy, who sit upon what at first glance appears to be a motorcycle—height, shape, the two large wheels. It is sleek. It has been carefully painted bright yellow. The handlebars appear to have been swapped out for an assortment of control sticks and levers. Pedals rise over each footguard. Visible beneath the bike's frame are car batteries, four of them in all, and lined with yellow lights.

The woman: "You satisfied now?" She sits in the sidecar on the left. The boy sits in the sidecar on the right. Like Crow, both are shirtless and wearing modified yellow hockey masks, some seemingly unified faction, the only glaring difference between the three of them being skin color. Strangely, neither woman nor boy face forward. Both are pointed backwards in their sidecar, small-caliber machine guns mounted for their use. Behind them—nearer to the front of the bike—are stationary riot shields bent at severe angles.

"Yip, sats'fied," Crow says. He hands the just-removed battery to the boy.

"The fuck m'I supposta do with this?" The battery is larger than his head.

"Make room," Crow says.

"I got some room over here, honey," the woman says. She stands, leans over the bike, her bare breasts sagging in front of the boy's face. Seconds after she takes the battery, Crow, straddling the bike, accelerates the three of them west, away from the lot, all origins of sound drifting north.

Vitri looks at Reyn and nods, then lifts himself back onto the passenger seat. Upon receiving approval, Reyn plunges her arm back beneath the driver's seat. Vitri opens his door and steps out onto the lot. Looks east. At fractions of the bridge. At the route he now believes they should give up on. *South it is*, he thinks. *South we go*.

He looks back at the Jeep. Reyn crawls over the center console and passenger seat. Once on her feet, she shows Vitri what she has found: a flashlight, no bigger than her hand. She clicks it on, revealing a white beam dulled by daylight.

Vitri nods. Squints at the street. "That's nice, Reyn," he says.

SOUTH, south for hours. Away from distant gunfire, out of the city's reach, into and across suburbs, past an airport with no planes or cargo, SOUTH, across desiccated creekbeds, where they eventually stop for soup and water, Vitri's eyes always east, SOUTH, off of the roads, into thinning forests, dried up bayous, even, swamp grass waist-high and feeble, ash beneath footsteps, merged into the grey and brown and yellow, SOUTH, until the sun sets, until night falls.

Vitri watches Reyn jackknife through the brush. Nimble, quick, gripping her backpack's straps, ducking beneath branches, glancing back every few steps, eyes in the night like two white buttons on a black shirt. She wants him to watch. Wants him to see her take the lead. Wants him to reconsider her.

"Slow down," he wishes he could say to her. "Stop trying to impress me."

Yet he *is* impressed. Pleased. And not just at how thus far he has underestimated her capabilities, her drive, but more so at the fact that she is not as thin as he'd originally surmised from the bagginess of her sweatshirt. He has to squint to see it now, but an hour or so ago, when, in the day's waning light Reyn forged ahead, he noticed a tightness of her jeans he hadn't before. Taut against the backs of her thighs. Shifting waistband halted at, and by, her developing hips. Enough to think her older than he did upon finding her. *Fourteen*, he thinks. *Maybe fifteen*, and accelerating now, taking charge, forging a narrow trail for the two of them.

Vitri stops for a moment when what he thinks is a spooked squirrel leaps from a nearby tree and onto the forest floor. He listens. To the twigs Reyn's feet snap ahead. To the rustling of the squirrel. And, before he continues, he hears the jangle of metal to his left, the pitter-patter of the squirrel bounding over hollow wood. Then it is gone, and Vitri only hears Reyn's steps, distant now, fading. He pulls his scarf down. Wipes the sweat from his cheeks and upper lip. Takes the flashlight from his pocket, clicks it on, white light hovering over the copper-tinted pine needles at his feet. Looks ahead, where he last saw Reyn. Slowly aims the light that way, hoping for her to see it, to turn back. When she doesn't, Vitri, knowing that Reyn will eventually look for him and see that he hasn't kept up, begins aiming the light elsewhere, searching for the origin of that hollow sound. He shrouds a trio of gouged tree trunks in light, gashes not made by saw teeth or bird beak, but a drill of some sort; several deep, thumb-wide holes line the trunks from left to right.

Vitri cautiously rotates the light over more matted weeds, more trees, more greys, and browns, and yellows. And then, in a small clearing no more than twenty feet from where he stands, he sees it: the white light shimmers off of a ground-level door latch. He squints. Steps through weeds, toward the clearing. Stops. Shines the door—fresh wood stained amber, a thin layer of dirt over its rusted latch.

Still no Reyn. No footsteps. No twigs.

It's a trap, Vitri thinks. He pictures a wire-rigged shotgun. A metal spike driven to his gut by hydraulics. Masked men and women sprinting to the sound. So he stops. Shines its perimeter, keen on locating the detonator. Sees nothing. Hears nothing. Thinks only of going back to the trail, of finding Reyn. Clicks off the flashlight and begins to do just that, turning around entirely, stepping through untouched weeds, stopping only when his right shin strikes something thin but sturdy, something immovable, stopping not because of how it feels, but because of the sound it creates, the quick burst of air. A tree branch snaps. Detaches. Falls to the ground. The door does not open; it's fired off, latch and all, eight feet into the sky, sparks trailing, leaving only a quick-to-fade afterglow on the hole's rim. Vitri draws the 9mm before the door crashes. Clicks on the flashlight. Aims both at the hole as he backs away, awaiting what comes next. But there is nothing. Nothing from that hole, nothing from beyond. A silhouette, a sound, for seconds there is nothing. So, flashlight still on, pistol still drawn, Vitri turns and locates Reyn's matted trail. Resumes his path. Sidesteps along, pistol still aimed at the hole. Further. Further.

And further. His mouth goes dry. His eyes water. He wheezes—soft at first, but harsher now, phlegm in the back of his throat layering itself. His vision fades. He stumbles forward. Falls to his knees. His torso constricts. Searches for more than water to send up and out. He crawls. Forward he crawls, leaving the dropped flashlight, the 9mm. Forward. Forward.

Between his attempts at breath he can hear it: liquid spilling from those gouged trees, spilling onto the leaves. Chemicals. Bitter on his tongue. Sour. Sharp in his lungs. But he crawls and, as he does, the wheeze evolves into a cough. *Crawl*, he thinks, *go, go-go-go, crawl, crawl, fucking crawl.* Twenty feet from where he fell. Twenty-five.

Thirty.

Thirty-five—

palm trees, a calm gulf, his wife slipping off a pink bikini, sashaying like a ballerina across white sand, toward him, towards their home, alone atop a gently-sloping dune, their son waving from a second-story window,

doo-doo-daahhh-dah-doo-doo-daahhh-dah,

Reyn appears alongside Carmen and, at first, she is smiling, her face no longer battered but full, cute, bronzed skin, cleaned teeth. But her smile soon fades. Trees appear, branches sawn, tops rounded like recently amputated arms,

109

doo-doo-daahhh-dah-doo-doo-daahhh-dah,

liquid spews from the trunk, onto Reyn, onto his wife, who falls to her knees and vomits onto each grain of darkening sand, torso locked, skin peeling, and Carmen is smiling, watching and smiling, smiling so wide, laughing now with Reyn's charred tongue

Water on his forehead, water on his cheeks, water on his lips, water on his chin, water beading to his neck. Vitri opens his eyes to see Reyn crouching over him, raincoat hood up, eyes wide, left hand tilting a bottle of water. Her right hand is on his chest, rising and falling as he does. After setting the bottle nearby, Reyn helps Vitri sit up, then clicks on the flashlight, guiding the light over the notebook on his lap.

YOU OK?

Vitri inhales. Exhales. Wipes the water from his face. Bends his knees. Wiggles his feet. Feels how soggy his groin is. Can smell the urine. Takes a deep breath. Nods.

CAN YOU WALK?

Vitri's mind begins its clamber back to cognizance. Questions flood. *How long have I been here? Are you hurt too? Has there been anyone else?* When Vitri reaches for the notebook, Reyn pulls away. Shakes her head.

CAN YOU WALK?

Vitri shifts his legs again. Bends his knees. Wiggles his feet. Nods. As soon as he does, Reyn sets the flashlight on the ground, places the notebook into her backpack, then, facing Vitri, extends her arms. Once Vitri latches on, she anchors her weight to her heels, anticipating a harsh tug toward the ground, a grasp at her forearms. But, soon enough, and with effort from both parties, Vitri is on his feet. Wobbly, but okay, upright and walking in the dark—one step south, two steps, three. Reyn catches up. Places the 9mm in his hand. Bounds ahead, turns, walks just ahead of him, smiling. For one-hundred feet they walk like this, she encouraging him as if he were a toddler.

110

One-hundred feet becomes one-hundred yards. Two-hundred. Vitri's wheezing eases. His legs loosen. Reyn turns, leads him under trees, through clusters of brush her feet have already trampled over, the occasional mole hole caught in the white light Vitri aims at the ground. Reyn increases her pace as they angle southeast, down a gentle hill leading to several more. Up-down, up-down they go for two minutes, three, a stale note of pine on the west-blowing breeze.

Before they reach what Vitri believes to be the last hill, Reyn turns. Watches his feet, his shins, his thighs. She then plugs her left thumb into the night sky, eyes quizzical, awaiting a response. As he walks toward her, Vitri nods. Wheezes. Does his best to shoo her forward, feeling as if he no longer needs to be checked upon. Reyn smiles, then crests the last hill, leaving Vitri to watch her waist disappear, her back, her shoulders, her neck. Down a twenty-five-foot decline she goes, into what Vitri, as he approaches, sees is a U-shaped clearing, trees on all but one side.

In the center of the clearing stands a dark one-story building. Thirty by eighty. Several doors, several small windows, a parking lot to the south with a large sign overhead, text facing the adjacent gravel road. Vitri's assumption that it had once been a hotel of some sort—at the least, some remote cabin, a bed and breakfast—is confirmed as he works his way down the hill and the numbers above each door become visible. #1, #3, #5, all odd numbers freshly painted on its northwest side. All windows boarded. *Someone lives here.* He clicks off the flashlight once Reyn, thirty feet in front of him and walking along the north side of the building, turns east, out of sight. *This is someone's home.*

Reyn's legs are partially lit by the caged red light above the seafoam door of #8. Above #6 is a caged yellow light. #4: purple. #2: green, each bulb free of caps, bottom ends instead coiled in copper wire. Stapled to the wall, Reyn knows the copper wire eventually straightens and, fed between the wall and #8's hinge, continues inside to copper mugs of nails, screws, washers, other chunks of metal. Having spent nearly ten minutes in #8, peering out the narrow gap of the boarded window, waiting—just waiting for any kind of danger, for any sign of the masked, Reyn knows that they'll be safe here, at least for tonight. She knows there are three more red lights on the other side of the door. A television, a table snug against chintzy green and yellow wallpaper. There is a bathroom. A cracked porcelain tub, a rusting showerhead, a toilet without water. She knows there's a twin bed to be shared.

When Vitri appears, Reyn's smile fades—the scarf is back on, tied tight; his pistol is drawn, gripped by both hands as he walks toward her. Not once does he lower that pistol. Not once does he glance at Reyn. Not once does he notice her waving arms, her shaking head. His eyes shift instead from the easternmost woods, to the half-lit patches of cement outside of each room, to the door of #8. Repeat. Repeat. Repeat. Until he nudges open the door and Reyn is left to watch him storm in, the pistol's definition a blur, appearing instead as an extension of his hands, his hands and arms an extension of his chest. He proceeds to probe the room. Tousles the quilt. Aims at each corner. Peeks around the bathroom door. Then, he looks at Reyn in disgust. Waves her inside and, as soon as her feet are out of range, slams the door. The copper wire fed through the doorframe fractures. The red light outside of #8 goes dark.

As Reyn sets each backpack on the bed, she is nudged aside by Vitri, who, having shoved his pistol back into his waistband, frantically unzips and tears into Reyn's backpack. Out comes the notebook. Out comes a pen. When he is finished writing, he tosses the notebook onto the bed.

WHAT THE FUCK ARE YOU THINKING?

In the red light, Reyn watches Vitri rip the scarf from his face. Watches him gulp from a plastic water bottle. Watches him pace the room. There are creases all over his face. Above his eyebrows, on the bridge of his nose, rippling across his forehead. And Reyn is confused. *You are no longer on the ground. We are no longer in the woods. There are four walls. We won't need to start a fire. We won't have to waste a candle, nor the batteries of the flashlight. There is warmth. There is warmth, and I brought you here, and I saved you, and—*

112

She offers the notebook to Vitri as if it were a delicate jewel she'd dinged, eyes down in apology, unable to help herself from flinching when Vitri yanks it from her hands. She glances at him as he reads. Watches him sigh. Watches him rub an eye with his left hand. When he sits on the bed, Reyn scoots as far away as she can, holding the pen out for whenever he is ready.

SOMEBODY LIVES HERE
YEAH
NO PROBLEM WITH THAT?
WE'LL LEAVE WHEN THEY WANT US TO
WE WON'T HAVE THE FUCKING OPTION
WE'LL BE SAFE HERE
THE MASKED WON'T NOTICE A LIT BUILDING?
WE'LL BE SAFE HERE
BULLSHIT
I WAITED. I WATCHED. I WENT BACK FOR YOU
DIDN'T SEE ANYTHING?
NO
DIDN'T SMELL ANYTHING?
NO
DID YOU HEAR ANYTHING?

Reyn's hands twist into fists. She picks up the notebook and throws it across the room, somewhere beneath the rage hoping that Vitri is right, that she did miss something, that, just so he can deal with the consequences of being right, there really is someone out there to hear the pages rip. She then kneels on the bed and shoves Vitri in the back as hard as she can, the first, the unexpected, being the most effective, Vitri's torso tilting sideways. But he braces himself. Tightens his core until Reyn's actions morph from shock to annoyance.

He shoves Reyn back. Once. Hard. Down she goes on the bed, wounded cheek crashing into a risen spring. She feels something in her throat, a tiny ball of energy evolving, expanding into something that can no longer stay, into something that she rolls its way up and off of her tongue. And then Vitri's hands are on her neck, fingers wrapped around that ball, pressing, pressuring, doing their best to cut it off. Once it's kneaded away, so go his fingers. So go his hands.

Seconds later, Vitri is off the bed. Reyn catches her breath, lifts her head high enough to watch him retrieve the notebook. As he turns around, Reyn, ferocity now tainted by terror, scurries as far away from him as she can, to the narrow headboard. When he is finished writing, Vitri walks toward the bed, ignorant of how Reyn braces herself for a blow. Sets the notebook next to her. Grabs a pillow. Plops the pillow on the floor, at the food-end of the bed. She waits until he lies down to read.

I THOUGHT YOU COULDN'T SPEAK
I CAN'T

Without rising from the bed, without even craning her neck to spot his exact location on the floor, Reyn tosses the notebook in Vitri's direction, then the pen. She hopes the spine nicks his chin, gashes it, leaves some sort of blemish, a bruise, a scab, a scar. In a matter of fifteen seconds, up the notebook comes at her, pages still bound but awry, altering its flight. Then comes the pen, tumbling through the air, end over end.

SCREAM AGAIN IF YOU SEE ANYTHING

An hour passes.

Reyn carefully buries her face into the pillow, back into the faint scent of cinnamon. This room, she has thought for a while now, belonged to a woman, who, based off of the strength of the room's remaining scents, was last here not that long ago. She pictures a husky woman with curly hair, but isn't sure why. A husky woman still valuing hygiene. Eucalyptus. Lavendar. A husky woman surviving here alone, spending her days rigging light fixtures. Reyn pictures a refrigerator in one of the other rooms, a freezer the husky woman stored underground, full of meat, the last of the strawberries she'd bartered for, the last of the cantaloupe—

—Reyn misses cantaloupe. Misses watching her father pare cores with sharp knives he'd smuggled from the restaurant. Misses opening her jaws wide and sinking her teeth in that soft orange flesh.

Another hour comes and goes.

Reyn, back pressed to the headboard, slurping soup she has taken from Vitri's backpack, rotates her eyes from the ceiling to the window. As muted as the red interior lights of #8 are, as tight as the boards have been nailed over the window, in slivers Reyn can see the sun yawning itself awake. Black to dark blue, dark blue to grey, lighter, and stretching lighter.

She is uneasy about the start of a new day, the previous unraveling entirely unlike what she imagined. She'd regretfully pictured the two of them holding hands while slogging through Shreveport, boarding Vitri's cousin's boat as one. Stopping not just when hungry or hurt, but just to stop, to converse, to plan, to laugh, to smile. Carrying on, at the very least, as friends. She wants to wake him up. Wants to ask him, CAN WE? CAN WE BE FRIENDS? She wants to know what happened in the woods. Wants to know whether or not he can confirm her worry, that her being deaf, that her lack of proper education, that her minimal exposure to those outside of her family, have all made it that much more difficult to read someone like him. Wants him to explain why she continues to imagine San Juan as a sliver of paradise. Wants him to tell her that he never saw his kiss serving as a catalyst.

Thinking of it in such terms makes Reyn think of her mother, that time she'd written, A KISS ISN'T TO CEMENT THE END OF SOMETHING, BUT THE BEGINNING.

Her mother had written it for Reyn's father. About him, his tendencies. Based on physicality alone, Reyn still wonders often how her father had been capable of capturing the attention of so many women. Thirty pounds overweight. Filthy. Scarred, and with little desire to correct any of it. Reyn found comfort in his posture, how, when he wasn't sitting or lying down, everything seemed to open up—shoulders back but lax, hands either on his hips or clasped behind his waist like a soldier standing at ease—as if it were an open invitation to approach, to judge if one must. It could also have been in the way he touched people, the warmth one could find in a man who would hold you for as long as you wanted, or in the security one could extract from his right thumb— never still, always rubbing—massaging a neck, the top of a hand, a shoulder. For all Reyn knows, her father possessed the sexiest voice in Monroe. He could've whispered often, leaned in close and tickled his listener's ear with propositions, with promises of some long-winded, multi-border adventure they'd never take.

However he'd done it, Reyn, from age twelve, up to the night preceding his departure, had watched her father walk those women back to the house. Amble, really, down that half-lit sidewalk, at 2:00am, sometimes 3:00. Passing a bottle back and forth. Colliding into one another and smiling about doing so.

It had been one woman per week at first, on Thursdays, his lone night shift. Within two months, he was working three night shifts: Tuesday, Thursday, and Saturday. At the conclusion of his night shifts. Reflecting on that first time, though, Reyn can't remember why she'd already been awake at such an hour, if she'd been reading, if she'd been writing, or if it'd just been one of the many nights that she lay in bed, eyes open, conscious brain spending its unsettled hours leaping from past to future, from future to past, to and from moments that felt normal, and necessary. What had anchored her to the present that night, she'd soon discover, was the flickering of light outside of her window. More than that, there was movement of that light: back, forth, back, forth across her window, in and out, in and out. So she'd risen and walked to that window. She'd pried two blinds and peeked out into the night. She'd seen her father's black work pants at his ankles, his splattered apron draped over his shoulder. One foot on the grass, one on the sidewalk, hips thrusting something small and stiff into the woman whose arms had been wrapped around the base of the streetlamp. She remembers the woman's hair—auburn under the light—and she remembers glimpsing the woman's eyes—wide, then closed, then wide again, either in pain or euphoria, neither of which young Reyn had the capacity to describe or decipher—and she remembers how two or three minutes later, up their pants had gone. They'd smiled. They'd laughed. They'd hugged. They'd sat on the grass and shared a cigarette, then stood, and kissed. And that was it. Off she'd gone, down the sidewalk, and in he'd come, with his bottle, more than happy to sleep blanketless on the couch.

Reyn remembers the thick black woman, hair beads swaying in the night, deflecting off of her chin and cheeks. She remembers the paperthin Nordic woman, her straw-colored eyebrows and hair. The Latin woman who didn't seem to want Reyn's

116

father to do any of the work, but bent over in the same spot as the rest of them, wrapped her arms around the streetlamp, and drove her backside into him. She remembers the night that Mr. Hirsham, a fifty-something single father of four, walked to the end of his driveway in a mauve bathrobe and, if Reyn had read his hand gestures correctly, asked her father and some young brunette with her paisley skirt flipped up to stop, to which Reyn's father responded with the tossing of a dark liquor bottle. She remembers the round-faced coworker whose black-framed glasses fell off of her face and onto the sidewalk, the left lens popping out, crushed by a footstep moments later.

She remembers them all. Their smiles. How often they brought each cigarette to their lips. How long they held the hug. How, afterwards, before her father would send them on their way, they'd all look at the house, eye every window not with concern or confusion, but with promise, as if they were certain their entrance was imminent, that what they'd just done ensured access they'd begun to desire. Reyn remembers never seeing any of them more than once.

There was another night that Reyn, rather bored with her father's routine—the initial shock and awe having been dulled by his silence and the minimal impact his actions had had on the way he treated her—and rather hungry, walked down the stairs, into the kitchen. And there her mother sat, at the bistro table near the back door. In the dark. Cigarette tip glowing. Initially halted by the image, Reyn eventually walked past her mother. Flipped on the light over the sink. Watched her mother wipe away tears, then grabbed a pad of sticky notes from the counter, and a pen.

> I SHOULD'VE TOLD YOU SOONER
> I'VE KNOWN LONGER THAN YOU

Which confused Reyn. She wanted answers. Truths she knew would only lessen guilt but stoke anger. *Why haven't you stopped him? Why aren't you out there? Why haven't you said anything?*

> HOW LONG?

Reyn's mother glanced at the question. And that's all it was: a glance, followed by a shrug. She then peeled the note from its pad and crumpled it into a crooked heap. Grabbed the pen. Wrote small.

HE WON'T BRING THEM IN HERE BECAUSE HE WON'T LET THEM INTO THAT PART OF HIS HEART

She stubbed out her cigarette. Continued.

HE LOVES US. WHAT HE DOES OUT THERE WON'T CHANGE THAT

Reyn's mother rose from the table. Rubbed her eyes. Adjusted the disheveled collar of her grey t-shirt, then stepped toward what from that point forward would be openly known as her bedroom, and only hers. But Reyn wrote, and Reyn followed, grabbing her mother by the arm and placing in her hand the night's final question:

ARE WE GOING TO LEAVE?

At which Reyn's mother smiled. Smiled and shrugged her shoulders, though not in what Reyn would classify as confusion, or in any manner fueled by the unknown, but rather in a manner of certainty. "Look around," her mother's shoulders said, "I can't."

Lying on #8's bed, Reyn feels as if she should've walked outside that night. Walked outside, interrupted her father, just grabbed his arm, brought him inside, and instructed him to enter that bedroom and kiss his wife. Something that said it starting again, or that it was over. That sent her in her own direction. Because Reyn's mother was incapable of moving on without someone else saying to her, GO. *Addict*, Reyn thinks. *Addict*. Not to that house. Not to comfort. Not to Ohapila. *Addict*: to Reyn's father. *Addict*: willing to become a tool, a pawn, something to be shoved around, used.

Addict: Reyn's father. *Addict*: to sex, to pain, to the chase of sex and pain, whether the journey be short and void of obstacles, or long, country-wide and tumultuous. *Addict*: not to his daughter, not to their house, not to his wife. *Addict*: to himself.

And what, Reyn has wondered often, could this possibly say about her? Does being the product of two intensely selfish people mean that her path has been laid out, that she has been doomed from the start? Can a dominant behavioral trait be reversed simply by recognizing the trend? Can it?

118

Can it?

Reyn sets the soup she has been sipping on the nightstand. Crawls to the foot-end of the bed. Watches Vitri sleep. Wonders if his COMPLICATED has placed him in a category adjacent to either of her parents. Wonders how many wives he has deserted. How many children.

Half an hour passes.

Reyn can feel the bedsprings recoil as she pushes herself off of the mattress. Once on her feet, she peers down at Vitri. Asleep, on his back, neck twisted to the side, mouth open. Chest: rising, falling, rising, falling. It pains her that Vitri won't make clear what he expects of her, what he wants the two of them to be—friends, lovers, or nothing. And so she's going to leave him, just like this, in peace, do them each a favor, and journey into the still-rising sun alone. She knows that he won't be concerned enough to request an explanation, but if he were to wake, and scramble, and present the notebook and pen with a look that asked why, Reyn would write: THANK YOU FOR WHAT YOU'VE DONE FOR ME. SAN JUAN WILL BE PERFECT.

Secure in her escape plan, Reyn, as stealthily as she can, walks to her backpack. She bends over and slowly unzips the largest pocket so that she can extract Vitri's pistol and lay it on the bed, a noise and movement that stirs Vitri. He sits up. Yawns. Swipes balls of green-grey gunk out of his eyes. Runs his fingernails through his greasy hair. Stands. Stretches his neck. Rolls his shoulders. Reyn unzips her backpack and begins to pull the notebook and pen back out of her bag, though, before she can, Vitri, feet planted, motions for her to stop. He turns his attention to the door, to, from what Reyn can tell, nothing. The door. Its deadbolt. Yet neither hint at what's on the other side—there's no jiggle, no denied turn of the knob, no tremors.

Vitri bends to the floor for his scarf and backpack, slipping each to what have become their natural resting spots on his body. He also grabs his pistol, readies it to fire, and rises as slowly as he'd bent, ears still attentive to the door, eyebrows angled in confusion. With his free hand, he motions for Reyn to stand, for her to put her backpack on, and then, for her to go to the door. Which she hesitantly does, tiptoeing past him, stopping only when he places his hand on her shoulder. Feet from the door: still nothing.

Vitri takes one step to the left of the doorframe, then imitates what he wants Reyn to do: stand where she is, turn the knob, pull the door open as quickly as possible, and hold. Reyn nods. Grips the knob. *This will be over soon.* Waits for the pistol to once again become an extension of Vitri's hands, of both outstretched arms. Waits for his look. *You'll leave him soon.*

Vitri nods.

Reyn turns the knob, yanks the door open—pinning herself between it and the wall, the only things in her line of sight being the bed, the television, the bathroom door—and holds. There's a flash, a wave of sound that follows, ending quickly enough for Reyn to feel Vitri's boot scrape across the door sweep, a slight careen into dawn. Seconds later, another flash. The sound waves from Vitri's pistol embed in her skin. Then, she sees a hand—his hand—reach around the door, presumably for her, waving her out of the corner. Tentatively, Reyn steps out and around, until Vitri can grab her sweatshirt. Out of #8 she is pulled, toward him, toward a thin black man with stiff silver hair lying on the pavement, clutching his shoulder. His eyes are shut. Mouth open, teeth clenched, interstate-like wrinkles up, down and across his bare arms. No more than ten feet from the wounded man stands two more men and one woman, all elderly, all with their hands in the air, all shivering. One of the two men—wearing a thin grey t-shirt and bent horn-rimmed glasses—blinks back tears. The other's skin looks like a used coffee filter, pale, stained, sagging. The lone woman, in a baggy white t-shirt with a red *American Queen* sewn over an image of a riverboat, refuses to look up at all, eyes only on her open-toed shoes.

Vitri is yelling something. Their hands linked, Reyn can feel it transmit through his fingertips. He is pulling her south. Three yards, four yards, across the burnt lawn, Reyn's feet failing to fully comprehend the situation, slow to match Vitri's long strides. Ten yards, fifteen yards. Reyn looks back to see the three huddled around their wounded, speaking to him, caressing his cheek. They do not give chase. They cannot give chase. They are brittle. They are too tired to harm, too wise. Left to struggle to move their fallen to comfort, to a bed, to his bed. *They're ruined.*

Reyn wrestles her hand free of Vitri's and, expecting him to react—to tackle, to shoot, to shout—unzips her backpack, extracting from it two cans of tuna. When she turns back around, Vitri is twenty feet ahead, pistol still in his hand, waving her forward. She wants to deliver those two cans of tuna. She wants to write to them how sorry she is, to pen THIS WAS MY FAULT, to offer explanation for the chaos. She considers the pistol, imagines handing it and the two cans of tuna over to the elderly. Safety. Sustenance. Reparation.

But she stares at Vitri. She stares and she doesn't know what she sees. Stares and doesn't know what exactly she wants to see anymore. Stares and wishes she understood what about him and his actions are compelling her to forget the idea of the pistol, set the two cans of tuna here, on the ground, and follow in his path. And maybe it's just her. Her body's instinct to survive. Her heart's inability to accept itself.

Late morning. Sun nibbles through fog. A breeze stirs. South again, Vitri leading, twenty yards ahead of Reyn, pistol still out. More woods, more birds startled from bare branches into the sky, more dried creekbeds, more yellows and browns and dull greens. A squirrel, skinny, heaving its heavy tail across scattered leaves. In the distance, a three-legged deer, still alert, still determined to evade the slightest threat.

WHY DID YOU SHOOT HIM?

Reyn looks up from the notebook to see that fifteen yards from her, and closing, is Vitri, scarf off, pistol in hand. *Run,* she thinks, *run now, anywhere, any way, to anyone.* Yet it is that same fear that keeps her still, that has her thigh twitching.

At first, all Vitri does is examine her. He squints at her bruised cheek. Thumbs her lips apart to view her tongue.

And Reyn is shaking.

After placing the pistol in his waistband, Vitri asks for the notebook. Plucks the pen from her hand, contemplates her question.

121

Before a confused Reyn can reply, Vitri takes the notebook back. Scowls at her as he hands it over. Takes out his pistol once more. Resumes his pace.

HURRY UP. WATER AHEAD

There is. The woods Reyn and Vitri walk through eventually lead to what was once a shoreline, what remains winding, river stains making it obvious where currents once ran. Near the shore are man-moved mounds of gravel, and stumps of oak and ash, each lending to the transitory smell here. Within days from a harsh winter to a late spring, uncut trees, shrubs, and grass playing catch-up. To the north, one hundreds yards from where Reyn and Vitri stand, is a riverboat tipped on its side, captain's deck pointed south. Water runs where it still can beneath the boat, through its multiple decks, its blue-trimmed windows, trickling into what the river, upon closer view, has become: a soggy six-hundred foot crevice layered like a robin's nest. Coarse grass woven with roots and twigs.

Vitri steps toward the riverboat. Reyn follows, eyeing the shattered rocking chairs and wooden tables that have fallen from the boat's promenades. An inverted porchswing is still chained to a lower deck's overhead pipe. The red paddlewheel on the boat's stern looks to be relatively intact, perhaps even functional, impact only misplacing the occasional chunk.

Closer now, Reyn pictures the boat upright, operating at full tilt, the river high, decks populated by men and women with eyes peeled for riverside wildlife but, resorting to observing the wake the crew creates when there's none to be spotted. The two large black pipes would be flapping steam into the sky instead of lying like conquered chess pieces. That paddlewheel would be turning, turning so fast, and it would be so bright in the sun, just painted, the boat's sides too, a glossy white instead of an off-grey, no longer covered in the soot and silt of a river bled dry.

AMERICAN QUEEN, Reyn can see now it once was called, white lettering on the black hull. MEMPHIS, TN. She considers the woman outside of #8. Her shoes. Her t-shirt. Wonders whether she and the rest were passengers, or merely scavengers that had rummaged through the remains of a souvenir shop. She glances at Vitri. The glance becomes a stare—he does not move; he does not blink.

Vitri's wife sits on a porchswing outside of the River Bar & Grill. She wears a lavish scarlet dress, thin straps taut against her collarbone, tied behind her neck. A matching shade of lipstick has smeared onto the rim of her martini glass. Beside her is a white plastic mask that, if placed, would cover cheek to cheek, from upper lip to eyebrow. In her sight is a churning paddlewheel and, beyond that, St. Charles, Missouri, a city prepared for night, the neon lights of boutiques and taverns just visible in the hour's fading sun. She can hear the honks of cars and buses miles off, the occasional whoosh of traffic on an unseen but nearby highway. Above her is the faint jetstream of an ascending seven-thirty-seven. Sunlight bends through trees plugged into riverbanks, growing large and strong and crooked. The river is high but calm, the boat's wake gently slapping the shore. She watches this. She listens to the flags on the top deck flap in the wind, then takes off her matching heels and sets them next to the white mask, feeling as if, in doing so, she will appear less bewildered, more certain of something.

Fellow *American Queen* passengers mingle nearby, speaking low but emphatically about the strength of their cocktails, the weather forecast they've studied on their cell phones, the relatives of theirs in Minneapolis that intend to show them the city once the *Queen* docks. Crewmembers in radiant white calmly scurry about, refilling drinks, asking the passengers how they are enjoying their trip. All smiles, all teeth, all likening it—the mystique of the river, the design of the boat, the company they keep—to a fairy tale.

Emerging from the propped wooden doors of the bar and grill is Vitri. His hair is cropped short, his face shaved clean. The dark blue polo shirt he wears has come untucked from his khakis. House whiskey sloshes in his short glass as he walks to his

123

wife, slowly, an anxious hand in his pocket, mauling the thin lining that this very action has already torn. But then he stops. Feet from his wife, he stops. He looks at her. He studies her. An awkward stare, but one of love—he loves this woman; he wants to stand this woman up; he wants to hug her, as a friend, as a lover, as a husband; despite where this discussion is bound to go, he'll want to stay with her on this porchswing, and he'll want to kiss her, and he'll want the two of them to watch the—

"You had to bring it up here," Vitri's wife says. She doesn't address him with her eyes. Watches the paddlewheel instead. Takes a sip from her martini. "Just had to."

Vitri sets his wife's mask and heels on the deck so that he can join her on the porchswing. "You would've reacted differently had I asked you somewhere else?"

Vitri's wife keeps her eyes on her glass.

"Well," Vitri says. He sips from his drink and looks out to the river. "It's out in the open now."

"I've told you dozens of times that kids are the last thing I want."

Vitri watches his wife sip her martini. He loves how that lipstick smear on the rim of the glass bothers her, how, because it does, she runs her thumb over it, again and again, and again. "You've never told me why, though. Have never talked about what makes it so scary for you, what makes it so *petrifying*."

Vitri's wife sighs. "Kids just want their fucking screens, you know? TVs, laptops, phones, tablets. *That* is their life. Don't give me that look. You know it's true. You've seen it. The only reason they want this, anything like this—" she raises her free hand as if it can, and does, encompass the entirety of the scene, the river, the sun, the air, "—it's so they can make whatever they see on their screens real. In some shared experience a ninja they control sneaks around a riverboat deck The next year, they bring a gun to a park. They join a gang."

Vitri knows this to be just an arm of what his wife feels, a weak extension of the issue's core. But he feels they're getting somewhere, that he must call out the absurdity, and in a way that doesn't spook her, settling upon: "You're jumping pretty fast."

"Things happen pretty fast."

124

"But what you're describing is a child without direction, without people that care. Look, you don't think our parents thought we'd ruin the world? You don't think they were scared?" Vitri places his right arm around his wife's shoulders. "We'll raise our kids differently. They'll work at the store as soon as they can. They'll hike. They'll see mountains. They'll go to farmer's markets. They'll ride their bikes long after they're eighteen, they'll—"

"They'll be shunned." She leans forward, away from her husband's consoling arm. "You're describing a scenario in which parents are the child's best friends. How cool is that? How healthy is that?"

"Mine were."

Vitri's wife sighs. "I just told you that was a different time."

"How so?" When his wife doesn't answer, Vitri continues, "Kids today are just as mean as they were back then."

"That's my point. There has been no progress."

"*My* point is that they'll have us. They'll have your parents. They'll have my parents."

"After they're sent back to Serbia?" Vitri's wife gulps the rest of her martini. The expression on her face says it was a struggle, says that she knew better than to say such a thing.

"We'll visit fucking Serbia then," Vitri says. "Jesus Christ. I don't know what you want me to say. I really don't. But I want a son, and I want to have that son with you. I want you to be his mother. That's what these rings mean, isn't it? That together we'll bring something into the world? Something new, something that has an opportunity to thrive?"

Silence.

Footsteps along the deck. Chatter from the fellow passengers. A butter knife clanging a glass; a toast being made.

"One son?" Her voice is dejected, focused on buying time. Brain wrestling with itself for a way out of this, for an easy segue into something brighter, something that allows each of them to win tonight.

"One son."

"No girls?"

Vitri laughs. "I couldn't handle another you."

Vitri's wife humors him by forcing a smile. Watches the river. "This son, what does he look like?"

"I don't know," Vitri says. He shrugs his shoulders. He thinks for a moment. "Fat, skinny, tall, short, blonde, brunette, it wouldn't matter. None of it would matter."

"And what if he's born disfigured? What if he comes out of me with only one foot? What if he has Down syndrome?" Vitri's wife swivels her body so that all of it—her chest, her legs, her eyes—are facing her husband. "What if he's deaf? Or blind? What then?" She lets her questions linger. "Because, if we were to have this son, if were to give life to this Roy or Billy or John, that's what I'd want, Vitri. I'd want him to not have to see what will become of the world." She waits for his eyes to shift. Watches him bite his lip. "A mother isn't supposed to want that for her child."

Somewhere inside the River Bar and Grill, a violin begins playing. *Doo-doo-daahhh-dah-doo-doo-daahhh-dah*, low, slow, sorrowful strings. A trumpet joins in, a trombone, a saxophone, until low and slow turns into high and fast, swinging, stringing into melody. The other passengers, the crew, all the smiles file inside, some of the women already swaying their drunken hips into their partners' groins. Vitri and his wife remain on the porchswing, neither appearing as if they intend to rise, eyes not on each other but directly in front of them. The paddlewheel. The river. The sun.

The *American Queen's* riverlorian, a stout man with shaggy hair named Hank, begins closing the propped doors of the bar and grill. He spots Vitri and his wife. "Come on, the ball's starting, you two," he says. His voice reeks of feigned excitement, an act, a veil over the disdain he has for such events, the regularity he plays in them, the ignorance it induces of the reasons he feels anyone should board this vessel. "I have your mask right here." This is true. In his right hand he carries one black plastic mask.

"Thanks Hank," Vitri says, "but it's too nice out here tonight to pass up."

Pleasure stretches across Hank's face before he says, "Have a good one," and closes the doors, a smile that shows how refreshing it is to him to see someone not so enthused over such a charade, but to be here for themselves, row hat can be found in the river.

For an hour or so more, there, on the porchswing, Vitri and his wife will remain, silent, and blank, tension static, stored, transferred to energy for when they nonverbally agree to table this conversation, stand and walk back to their suite, for when they throw themselves into one another—her face pressed against the wall, his hands so tight around her thighs.

###

Eventually, and without signaling to Reyn, Vitri turns from the *American Queen* and walks south, taking giant strides along the shore, peering at the enveloped river. He grabs an oblong chunk of wood and pokes the top layer, dragging grass and pine needles aside. Reyn walks to Vitri and watches him press the tip of the wood down further, through the second layer. In a matter seconds, something leaps from the water and snaps shut on the wood. Vitri holds tight. Yanks the chunk of wood out. On its tip: a bear trap, clamped, divots gnawed from each side.

Reyn watches Vitri toss it all to the river, then grab another chunk of wood from the gravel. As they walk south, Vitri drags more and more grass from the top layer of the river, exposing the remains of carp and catfish. Several more traps—bear, fox, coyote.

###

Despite having enough to last the night, Reyn, crooked arms already overflowing, continues to search the shoreline for more wood.

Seated on a tree stump by the fire, Vitri swivels to watch her bend, and crouch, her jeans inching further down her hips each time she does so. He sips the last of the tomato soup, then fills the empty can two-thirds full of water. He grabs a chunk of wood from the pile nearest him and, with it, shifts the burning logs. Flames leap from one log to the next, burning through dark green for seconds before settling on orange. Blue-grey smoke spurts into the air.

He sets the soup can in the gap he has created on the fire's floor, atop of and surrounded by glowing coals. There, the water will warm, will become a vehicle of his resetting, of feeling human for the first time in days. To scrub the soot from his face. The grit out of his beard. The blood off of his hands.

Reyn unloads her armfuls of damp wood, then half-circles the fire to sit on a shorter tree stump, away from Vitri. He's still unsure of how to register her continued avoidance. Moments of guilt have crept in since the night before, particularly following coughing fits. *Too hard on her.* Guilt for not apologizing, for not saying thank you, for not acknowledging her efforts. Yet those brief, potent moments have been swallowed by pride, by the satisfaction that has come from forcing this separation, from signaling to her that they are not to be romantically linked, from making clear that, yes, this will end, and, no, neither party should be paralyzed with sadness when that hour comes.

The two mix as Vitri watches Reyn struggle to remove the raincoat, sweatshirt lifting while she does so. A glimpse of hip flexors. Flat stomach. Ribs. Bellybutton. All strung tight. He watches until she settles, until he can feel her eyes on him. He looks away. Watches the fire. Pokes the flame. When his eyes drift back to her, he cannot tell what her face is saying: wounded, yes, quiet, humbled, but on edge, sad yet somehow optimistic, lips curling into the tiniest of smiles, some unique blend of resiliency he wishes he had a camera to capture, something that seems to say, "Throw everything you have at me, Vitri. I'll move forward." In the picture, bruises would be mended, and cuts. He'd ask her not to wear makeup, but to pull her hair back into a ponytail, to get those strands out of her eyes and off of her cheeks.

WHEN WATER IS WARM, I'M GOING TO WASH UP

Vitri shows Reyn the boxed bar of soap he has pulled from his backpack. A delicacy, Vitri thinks, one that he's willing to share. But Reyn feigns interest. Humors him by nodding. And it confuses Vitri, it offends Vitri to the point of feeling challenged, to the point of finding a topic upon which they each have something to say.

YOU SPOKE BACK IN THAT ROOM—YOUR VOICE IS STRONG

Reyn reads. Nods. Nods as if she knows, as if she has always known but has opted for utter silence. Hands the notebook back. Stares at the fire.

HEARING YOURSELF TALK ISN'T ALL IT'S CRACKED UP TO BE.

Reyn smiles at the self deprecation he happily delivered. A breakthrough. Invested once more, she reaches for the pen.

WHAT DOES YOUR VOICE SOUND LIKE?

Vitri says, "Tallahassee" and "Carmen" over and over, each time slower, dragging out the words, splicing syllables never intended to be there.

LOW, DULL, BORING
FIGURED

Reyn smiles at her joke as she hands Vitri the notebook. Seconds later, she is on her feet and walking behind Vitri. She takes the scarf from his neck, then gently places her chilled fingers around his throat, fanning them from clavicle to larynx, searching for a sound.

"Goddammit, you're never going to leave, are you?" Vitri says, fighting the tingling sensation escalating in his groin, up through his core. "Stop. Stop. Don't do this." But he doesn't fight her. He shuts his eyes, thinks of the last time he has been touched like this. So gently. So curiously. Thinks and settles on a time before the blackout. A bonfire in their backyard, his wife, tipsy from wine, taking a seat on his lap. Stroking his cheek as if it were the first time they'd ever been that close, achieving intimacy in front of a small crowd.

As if she were through untangling the intricate wiring of his throat, Reyn takes her hands off of Vitri. Back to her tree stump she walks, smiling, sore cheek stretched as far as it can go. Back to the notebook.

THERE ARE LAYERS TO YOUR VOICE. DEEP, QUIET. IT'S NICE
THANK YOU
YOU'RE WELCOME

As the flame transitions to dark blue, there are several popping noises within the fire, a click, a clack, similar to that of a tongue exploring its confines—its teeth, its lips, its cheeks. For Vitri, they are welcome noises, something to erode the silence, the brief moment of nothing between he and Reyn. No writing. No shared gaze or glance. He instead eyes the soup can, hoping that the process can be reduced to mere minutes, that steam will soon struggle into the sky.

YOU WANT TO WASH FIRST?
I DON'T NEED TO
IT'LL MAKE YOU FEEL HUMAN AGAIN

Reyn shrugs her shoulders. She guides loose hair behind her ear. Props her undamaged cheek with her palm. Anxious. Contemplative.

YOU GO FIRST

Vitri reads. Nods. Rises. Grabs the boxed bar of soap with one hand and extracts the soup can with the other. Around the fire he walks, and into the woods, twenty feet in, past wilting shrubs, past thin grey brush, to a tree stump on the fringe of the fire's glow. He places the soup can upon the stump and looks back. Confirms that the foliage will provide at least partial cover from Reyn. Proceeds to remove his boots and socks, setting them aside in their respective pairs. The big toe on his right foot is crooked, purple, and swollen, but he does not know why, cannot pinpoint where or when its cause occurred, or, more importantly, how; pain comes only now, gazing upon it in confusion. He runs his fingers along the bottoms of his bare feet. Cuts. Blisters, some anxious to burst, others popped and awaiting the removal of dead skin in order to regrow.

Next goes the raincoat, the sweater, and the grey t-shirt beneath. And, for the first time in days, Vitri looks at his bare torso. Pale, irritated, nipples raw, thumb-sized rashes purple in the night, chest and belly hair matted. With how loose his pants have become, he spots sea green veins running thick through his abdomen and over his hips. He hasn't seen such veins since he was nineteen and preparing for a cannonball into Lake Brazos. Fit. Young. In control. Pride has always come with these veins—he straightens his back, puffs his chest, eyes them at different angles—and memories. He feels his mind tiptoeing toward the last day he, the boy, and his wife put on their swimsuits. Ten months ago. Hot. 111-degree hot. Their neighborhood: abandoned. Hope: fading.

"We can't just sit here," Vitri had said to his wife.

"That's what I've been saying for how long?" Vitri's wife: exhausted. Sleepless nights of gnashing teeth. Almost two weeks without bathing.

Vitri refused to acknowledge her rhetorical question, refused the satisfaction she'd get with yet another discussion about leaving Waco. "We can't just sit in this house, all day, every day. There are still things to do right outside our door."

They had then asked the boy what he'd like to do. "Anything you want," they'd said. He'd emphatically opted for swimming.

"Swimming it is."

Six doors down they'd gone, to the Kendricks'. They'd walked across the front yard. They'd let themselves in through the pool's gate. As a family, they'd approached the pool ledge. As a family, they'd seen the litter of kittens bobbing in the water. Calico fur, orange fur, pure black. Vitri had hurried to the gate, grabbed the nearby net, fished them out in front of his wailing son, then—

Vitri fights the memory. Curls his toes into the forest floor; feels leaves crumbling in their vise. *Those moments no longer exist.* He lifts the soup can from the stump and dunks his fingers into the water. Brings his fingers to his left armpit, swipes up, down, across. Then the right. Then his face and neck and hair. Applies soap until suds run from his head to his chest, and down, to his waistband, where it soaks through to his underwear. He shivers. Tingles. Shuts his eyes. Breathes in the cool scent of the soap. He unbuttons his pants and proceeds to scrub the left side of his penis, the right, the top, the tip.

###

Reyn stares at the still-evolving flames. Rubs her fingers along the forearm gooseflesh that, no matter what she tells herself, won't go away. *Don't look at him. He hates you. He hates you so much.*

When she gives in, when she finally does look at Vitri, his back is arched. His eyes are skyward. His right arm is chicken-winged and moving in rhythm—backward, forward, backward, forward, backward, forward, until his pants drop to his ankles and he stumbles to a nearby tree trunk, left arm extended to prop himself. Reyn stands. Cranes her neck not in wonder, but in worry, that, like last night, he soon will be on the ground, in need of water, in need of rescuing. But then his right arm moves faster—backward-forward-backward-forward-backward-forward-backward.

Until he shivers. Until his back eases. Until the arm stops. And then he bends over. Pulls his pants up. Looks back. Sees Reyn. Stomps into his boots and, in one quick, imprecise movement, grabs all that he has temporarily discarded—the shirt, the sweater, the soap, the can—and walks toward the fire.

Reyn sits on her stump. Keeps her eyes on the flames until Vitri, still shirtless, is feet from her, pouring more water into the soup can. After setting the can back near the flame, Vitri puts his shirt on, then the sweater. He pulls from his backpack another pair of socks and, once he has slipped them on, one almond-scented candle. To light the wick, he straddles the fire and inches it close to a low-burning flame, water dripping from his hair and chin and onto the coals.

Once back on his stump, Vitri holds the candle close to his nostrils. Then, as if just realizing that Reyn is still there, across from him, he looks at her and smiles. Smiles wide. His face is different now. Relaxed. Eyes open, but drooped just so, loose, free. He sets the lit candle on the ground and reaches for the notebook.

I'M GOING TO TAKE A WALK
RIGHT NOW?
BEST TIME
OK
WASH UP. I'LL WAIT FOR YOU
YOU DON'T HAVE TO
I'LL WAIT. GO ON

Reyn's heart races. She does not want to go for a walk. She does not want to wash herself in his view. What she wants to do is sit right here, on this stump, look Vitri in the eye, and shake her head no. He hovers over her, arms extended, handing over the cold soup can and the bar of soap. "Go on," his eyes say, "go ahead."

Not understanding but attempting to respect just why this is of the utmost importance to him, Reyn hesitantly takes the items and, sloshing water as she does so, hurries to the treeline, looking back only to determine where she must go to be entirely concealed. Only when there are two modest oaks directly between she and Vitri does she set the soup can and soap on the ground. She intends to leave them there, to not touch them, to just stand here, counting the seconds as she kicks loose leaves, dabbing water on her face and hair before returning to the fire. Feigning it all. Plans that, when peeking around the tree trunk, seem as if they would be successful—Vitri is occupied, eyes shut, candle beneath his nose—but plans that disintegrate as Vitri's eyes open and dart to her. Reyn turns. Backs herself against the tree trunk. *You'll leave at first light, you'll leave at first light, you'll leave at first light.* Furiously removes her shoes and socks. Yanks off her sweatshirt without consideration of her wounds, tosses it on the ground. Dunks her fingers in the soup can, swipes her armpits first, and quickly. The tops of her feet, between her toes. Then her neck, cold water drizzling to her chest, soaking through her t-shirt and bra. More water. A scrubbing of her hair, of her face.

That's enough, Reyn thinks. *That's plenty.* Before she puts everything back on, she once again peeks around the tree trunk. What she sees now is Vitri storming toward the woods, toward her, working to unbutton his pants as he does so.

She wants the pistol from her backpack; she wants RALPH's sickle; she wants to run. And she does. Barefoot, she does. She takes off, away from Vitri. Ten-fifteen-twenty feet before looking back. Vitri, who had given chase, is now slowing. Coughing. Hands searching for a scarf that isn't there. He staggers to a halt before falling face-first into the dirt.

Reyn slows. Waits to see if he will push himself up, push himself forward, to the side, push himself somewhere. But there he stays, body backlit by the fire, his back rising, falling, rising-falling, quicker and quicker. Wary of this being some trick, some strange way to lure her, Reyn continues to watch Vitri. Rise-fall, rise-fall. Waiting for either his body or his will to expire. For moments Reyn stares, until, overcome only with what she can classify as pity, she slowly approaches, questioning each step, batting *Leave him* and *Help him* between her ears. When she is within ten feet, Vitri stirs. Barely rolls himself over. Upside-down, he searches for Reyn. Locates her. Tries to wave her over. Reyn stays put, watches his hands, judges the severity of this. *Why help you?* Steps closer. And closer. Sees him motioning for what she interprets as, "water," a request she decides she can accommodate. Reyn walks to the soup can she left, grabs it, and returns to Vitri, setting the soup can not in Vitri's hand, but nearby, within reach. She backs away. Watches him clamber to the can, watches him tilt it, watches the water splash on his face. She glances from Vitri, to the fire, and back, wondering not whether she could help him get there, but if she should, a question answered by the pain in her tongue, the constant reminder of why she's still breathing. *You owe him*, she thinks. Reyn steps closer. And closer. *Just him to the fire, then leave.*

Reyn slides her hands beneath Vitri and helps him roll to his stomach. Grabs the back of his sweater, anchors her weight to her heels, and helps lift him to his feet, quickly side-stepping herself beneath his arm before his quivering becomes severe enough to drop him back to the ground. Together, they turn around, Face the fire. Step forward. One step, two steps, three, Reyn feeling his breath as they do so, its pace, the warmth of his pulse, feeling through his arm his attempts to speak. She glances at his mouth: "   , Reyn.   need   you. I need   you."

Vitri points to leaves and grass off the edge of the tree line. Nods as if it is where he wants to be left. And so Reyn obeys. Helps him there. Waits for him to lift his arm from her shoulders and descend. But the arm is never lifted—as Vitri goes down, so too does Reyn, falling on top of him, flailing, writhing, fighting, and fighting, and fighting, but going nowhere. She can feel his words on her ear, can feel his lips on her neck. Doesn't want his hands on her breasts. Doesn't want them unbuttoning her pants, doesn't want them slithering beneath the elastic band of her underwear.

Vitri's fingers search for the grip of the 9mm. He draws the pistol but he does not aim it. The scarf is over his nose and mouth. His eyes are forward, squinting into the grey light of dawn. Five hundred yards ahead, atop a gradual slope, are one-story buildings. Buildings just built. There is the faint echo of hammer and nail, the occasional glimpse of an unmasked man walking alongside the structures. Vitri steps forward, the initial blend of confusion and terror quickly morphing to intrigue. But he stops once more. Watches. For moments, just watches. Listens to a small engine start.

###

Reyn wakes naked and alone, blood on her teeth and gums. Grass sticks to her hair and back. Flakes of her tongue clog her throat. Untended for hours, the fire is now a heap of blackened wood, single strands of smoke dissipating in a cloudless sky. She sits up. Slides on her underwear. Clasps her bra. Stands. Walks into the woods to retrieve the rest of her clothes, not once craning her neck, not once looking for Vitri. Because, sometime in the night—while beneath him—she'd told herself to expect this.

As she does now, Reyn had thought then of the last time she saw her father. Actually saw him. Smelled him. Watched him. Wanted to hug him. She remembers that he'd risen earlier than usual for a breakfast shift, where she suspected he'd angrily flip pancakes, over fry eggs and intentionally burn white toast. INSULT TO MY TALENT, he'd written to her once, on a similar day, to which he followed with: ONLY + IS HAVING AN ENTIRE NIGHT TO WASTE. More often than not, she knew, this was a lie, a fib, an exaggeration, Reyn's father returning home immediately after his shift, exhausted, unable to stay awake for dinner, choosing instead to lie on the living room floor, apron still on, hands laced over his gut. Something about the dinner rush, though, contrarily seemed to invigorate her father, ignited him into giving that street lamp a second purpose.

Yet, on that particular night, Reyn remembers her father walking into the house sometime between six and seven, half-turned and smiling, right arm extended and pulling through the doorway a petite woman with straight purple hair. She, too, was carrying an apron and she, too, smiled and she, too, looked at Reyn. And she waved. Which confused Reyn. Never had she seen this woman. Never had her father insisted upon her, or any of them, entering the home he shared with his daughter and wife. Though her mother was not in sight, Reyn, if she knew her as she thought she did, pictured an empty desk. An open back door. An overflowing ashtray on the rotting

135

deck. Not in sight, but somewhere nearby, too scared to run away, too scared to confront.

In that moment, however, Reyn, as cruelly as she could, waved back. Stiff hand up, stiff hand down. Because she was supposed to hate this woman. Regardless of hair color, regardless of clothes, posture, smile or frown, she was supposed to want her out of here, this *slut*, this *whore*, this *bitch. Out*, she was supposed to think, *get out of this house. Stop hurting my mother*. She was supposed to hate her father. *Pig. Scoundrel. Prick. Asshole*. Four words fluttering in her mind, but so intangible were they, so elusive, unable to be communicated by her even if grasped by a searching hand. There was just so much joy in him, something he'd openly transmit to Reyn when around, something she thought foolish to look at, feel, and then deny, carrying on either in anger or envy. So, the best she could do on that night was look away. Ignore his happiness, ignore her, ignore them as much as possible—an abandoned tactic when Reyn, lounging on the sofa in sweatpants, caught out of the corner of her eye her father's pointing finger.

Don't, Reyn thought, *no. Just don't. Don't bring her over here. Don't put me in that position*. She waited for the inevitable, for the two of them to enter her line of sight, for her father to frame the purple-haired woman as if she were a prize he'd won at a carnival. For the purple-haired woman's mouth to flap a futile introduction. She looked down. Waited. Five seconds. Ten. Twenty. She waited until caked dust pirouetted from the staircase's railing to the floor, until she could see the stairs bow under her father's steps.

When Reyn looked back at the front door, there still was the purple-haired woman, clutching her purse, anxious eyes on her black server sneakers, unsure of what she was to do, unsure of what was to happen next, the likelihood of this work-fling amounting to anything, the validity of this family's arrangement, whether or not Reyn's mother would emerge from a bedroom or closet with a knife or screwdriver. The image was enough to spur concern from Reyn—perhaps she, too, was partially responsible for the anxiety, lounging there on the sofa, standoffish to the fearful woman at the door. A tumor of sympathy began to swell in Reyn's stomach and, though she could opt to leave the living room altogether—sprint upstairs, to her father, to her bedroom, to that deck, that overflowing ashtray—within seconds Reyn was waving the woman over.

Registering as brown from a distance, Reyn could see that the woman's eyes, now under light, were closer to burnt orange; *a perfect compliment*, Reyn would think later, to that hair, to those dark eyebrows, to that silver hoop through her bottom lip. Despite the odor of fried food, Reyn could smell the melon-scented perfume on the woman's wrists as she sat down. Faint, but noticeable. Despite exposure to splattering grease and fluorescent bulbs, her skin was smooth, and glossy, presumably prioritized ahead of her stained teeth when it came to hygiene. As she sat down, the purple-haired woman pulled from her purse a notepad the size of her hand. Then, a pen. She smiled as she wrote.

I'M FAYE

In addition to thinking the name pretty, and fitting, Reyn believed Faye's handwriting to mirror the way in which she carried herself—she either didn't believe in, or was incapable of, straight lines, even the vertical line in her I curved, elegant.

I'M REYN
I KNOW. YOUR FATHER CAN'T STOP TALKING ABOUT YOU
WHAT DOES HE SAY?
TELLS ME HOW SMART AND PRETTY YOU ARE

Reyn pictured her father weaving around dishwashers and prep cooks, chatting up his daughter. She pictured him on break, puling out his cell phone, waving the servers behind the line to show them the pictures of her reading, the pictures they'd taken together—at the aquarium, in front of the otter exhibit, at the very top of a Ferris wheel. In doing so, Reyn's cheeks began to tingle, to warm. Flattered that the words SMART and PRETTY had been used but embarrassed, with wonder, at the prospect of CAN'T STOP TALKING ABOUT YOU.

WHAT ELSE?
HOW THOUGHTFUL YOU ARE. HOW GLAD HE IS THAT YOU'RE WHO YOU ARE

Faye must've seen Reyn's worry over the matter, or felt it, understood it enough to smile as she asked for the pen back.

ALL GOOD THINGS, SWEETIE. ALL GOOD THINGS

In which Reyn found comfort. Warmth found her cheeks. A grin took hold of her lips and eyes.

Though Reyn asked for her to elaborate, the request was met by a shoulder shrug from Faye. And, from there, their conversation took a nosedive when it came to substance. Faye's favorite color, Reyn found out, was, unsurprisingly, purple. She was twenty-six years old. Originally from New Orleans. Mother to one calico tomcat. Filler. All filler. Faye knew it was. Reyn knew it was. But, as Reyn saw it, it was the best thing to happen to her in that house for a long time. An informed outsider had entered, sat down, and had been patient enough for ten minutes of written small talk—an effort that made Reyn feel as if she had a friend outside of these walls. An effort that, when Reyn's father descended the last stair and turned toward the living room, doused her heart in sadness—this, Reyn understood then, would be the only time Faye stepped foot in this house.

What made Reyn so certain was something beyond his slicked hair, beyond the clean-shaved face, beyond the khakis, beyond the tucked plaid button-up and dark brown loafers. It wasn't even his smile. It was in how Faye's smile mirrored his. Absolute joy, a reciprocal joy that neither Reyn or her mother could share with him. An understanding that need not be spoken, written, or realized pants-down at a lamppost. As if he were a model at the end of her runway, Reyn's father stopped near Faye, and playfully placed his hands on his hips before performing a spin. He looked at Reyn. Exchanged words with Faye. He then asked for the notepad and pen, passing it to Reyn once he was through.

WANT TO GO TO THE MOVIES?

Reyn wanted to. Wanted to nod her head, leap from the sofa, sprint upstairs, change, and sprint downstairs, to her father, to Faye, to the car, into the theatre, where she would watch them, and only them, not needing subtitles, not needing narration of any sort, inference and intuition more than enough to make sense of what was in front of her.

Before Reyn could do any of that, before she could even nod, her father turned. Faye turned. And there, between them, walking through the dark dining room was Reyn's mother. Slowly, arms crossed, mouth moving, eyes scanning the three of them. Guilt and panic collide and expand within Reyn, shoulder to shoulder, waist to throat. She watched Faye snatch the notepad and put it back into her purse. Saw her father straighten his back and puff his chest. Watched calm turn into chaos. Strained necks. Overworked jaws. Stamping feet. Screams. Arms and hands structuring individual arguments, deflating all others. And Faye, eyes down, more than just her feet guiding her to the front door.

Reyn eventually did sprint upstairs, to her room, but only to watch Faye and her father walk hand-in-hand down the street after Reyn's mother chased them off of the yard. When her father didn't return the next day, or the next, or the next, or the day after that, Reyn knew that he was gone. Gone, gone, gone. And, each day afterward, she forcefed herself the idea that he and Faye were in love, that they had mutually realized that love, and that they'd ran off together to celebrate that love, to prove that love, to consummate that love. *All good things*, Reyn thought. Revisited. Justified. Clung to. A thought, however, that would be disproved when, months from then, days after her mother drowned the Idaho postcard, stopping at a gas station that had within days of the blackout been sucked dry, Reyn spotted a purple-haired woman slumped against an overflowing dumpster. Faye had died wearing a violet leather jacket and white pants. Bootprints were up and down her legs. Burnt orange eyes for all to see.

It isn't a mystery to Reyn why she thinks of Faye now. Her thighs ache. Saliva and wind have made her neck and nipples raw. Shards of pain stretch from groin to abdomen as she steps toward her sweatshirt. She has been abused, abandoned, trampled. She has been raped.

A ginger-colored squirrel watches dress from a low-hanging branch. The box of bar soap has been shredded, the bar itself nibbled, corners rounded, flies, beetles and whatever else staking their claim.

After stomping into her shoes, Reyn turns to see Vitri sitting by that charred wood heap, atop the same tree stump as the night before. Backpack: on. Scarf: on, and tight. Eyes: down. Thumbs: twirling. Pistol: on his lap.

Grab your backpack, Reyn thinks. She wills herself to the fire site, staring at Vitri as she does so, unsure of what exactly she and her pain-slouched body are expressing but hoping with every ounce of her that it will be interpreted by Vitri, should he have the nerve to lift his eyes, as something between rage and disappointment. *Grab your fucking backpack and leave.* She walks to her backpack and struggles to hoist it over her shoulder. It's when Vitri sets his pistol on the ground, rises from the tree stump and steps toward Reyn—presumably to help her—that Reyn's thin film of control is torn by the same fury she felt before JOHN went beneath the Jeep. Swiftly she unzips the largest pocket of her backpack and wraps her fingers around the handle of RALPH's sickle. Points the blade at Vitri. Dares him to take just one more step. *Just one more step.*

Whether it is the sight of the blade, or what it is he sees in Reyn's face—the enlarged eyes, the flared nostrils, how she continues to grip and regrip that thing, tighter, tighter, and tighter yet—Vitri stops. He raises his hands. Takes a step back. And another. And another, until he rediscovers that tree stump.

They stare at one another, Vitri changing posture only when Reyn breaks eye contact. He holds up his right hand, shapes his fingers as if they were holding a pen, scribbles in the air.

Reyn shakes her head.

He scribbles in the air again as if his initial message weren't received. But Reyn knows what he wants to write. He'll write what his deflated eyes feign: I'M SORRY. He'll write, and she'll read, and he'll expect her to forgive, to forget, to stay by his side, to provide him with what he thinks he needs. *No. Never again.* But she wants that SORRY. Wants to see his hand shake as he writes it. Wants him to not want to write at all, but to set the notebook down and embrace her. She wants to feel his tears on her shoulder. Needs to feel them. So she sets her backpack down. Exchanges the sickle for her pistol and holds it loosely in her left hand. She plunges her right hand back in for the notebook, which, still crouched, she flings at Vitri as hard as she can. The pen next, and then she stands. Takes pleasure in watching Vitri pluck the pen from the ground and situate the notebook on his lap, pleasure abruptly replaced by disappointment, at how easily his words bleed onto the page.

THERE'S A TOWN. THIS SIDE OF THE RIVER. TWO MILES SOUTH

Reyn reads. Lifts her eyes. Lowers them, reads once more. Contemplates dropping the notebook at her feet and backing away, pistol aimed at his throat so he won't follow. Looks at his eyes; sees what she seeks in each. *He wants to say it.* She shoves the pistol in her waistband, reaches for the pen. *He's going to say it.*

THAT'S ALL YOU HAVE TO SAY?
PEOPLE THERE. NO MASKS. BUILDING SOMETHING. HEARD AN ENGINE

Reyn emphatically draws an arrow to THAT'S ALL YOU HAVE TO SAY? She delivers the notebook, steps back, re-grips the pistol.

I WANT YOU TO GO WITH ME

Reyn shakes her head. Raises her arms. Fights tears as she circles her words.

THEY'LL HAVE A PLACE FOR YOU. THEY'LL HAVE FOOD, MAYBE BOOKS
THAT'S ALL YOU HAVE TO SAY?
DON'T CRY

She wishes she could stop, wishes that her inclination instead was to swap the pistol for the sickle and slice off each of Vitri's fingers, wishes she could render his hands useless, unable to write to her, unable to tell her in so many ways how worthless she is to him, something to be manipulated, to be discarded, to be dropped off when he's had his fill. She wishes she could force the tears back to her eyes, wishes Vitri would sit back on the stump, wishes that he'd just kept walking this morning, away from her, on and on and on and on, that he hadn't come back with news of a town that all at once could and would at once crush and excite her, the prospect of others, of Vitri dropping his unwanted goods off into the hands of people vastly unlike Vitri, warm people that wouldn't see her as worthless, kind people, nurturing people.

I'M SORRY

141

Vitri holds the notebook steady as he steps closer and closer. He stops three feet from her and studies her, for five seconds, for ten seconds. He tosses the notebook to the ground and reaches his hand toward her. Reyn swats his forearm away. Grits her teeth. Raises the pistol. Shoves the barrel into his chest and walks him back to the stump. She motions for him to sit.

South. South again. South, for just a bit longer. South, for the last time, along the shore, under a clear sky, Reyn with her raincoat on, pistol drawn but barely aimed at Vitri, yards in front of her. A dozen feet from her, a kingfisher dives into what had been the river, its beak slicing through the topmost layer. But that is all. There it stays, spindly feet twitching.

Reyn watches the kingfisher's legs go motionless. Carries herself forward, grimacing with each step. She hates this pain. She hates that she can watch something as sad as that kingfisher's unnecessary death and feel nothing. Hates this shoreline. Hates this river. Hates that she's walking south. Hates that she still holds the pistol. Hates that she doubts she'd even use it. Hates that she questions her every action. Hates that, at any given moment, she can turn around and walk north, or veer west. She hates that she hasn't, that she has allowed herself to be led by Vitri to what for upwards of two miles now she has wondered was yet another lie, another trap. *There is no town.* She hates herself. *You think you know what you're chasing after.* Hates how pathetic she is. How desperate for attention, for recognition, for love. She hates how much she has sacrificed for any of it.

So Reyn stops. Right there, she just stops, and sighs. She watches Vitri continue south. *You have no idea.* She takes a deep breath as she watches Vitri, the smell of mold breached momentarily by something faint but sweet, berry-like. Forty-five yards are between them now, fifty, his eyes on the gravel, shoulders somewhat slumped. Wonders if he notices the absence of her footsteps. Wonders if he continues anyway because he too knows that she and him should've split well before this moment. She wonders if any part of him would miss her. Fifty-five, sixty. Sixty-five. Reyn looks east, across the

142

still river. Trees framing moderate clearings, gradual yellow hills rolling into faint shades of green. She looks west. Woods. Thicker woods. Thicker trees, straighter trees, healthier trees than she has seen in some time, sickly grey and yellow leaves punctuated by small green ovals and spades, a path begging to be made through the budding fescue.

There is enough distance between she and Vitri now that Reyn could blot his body out with a raised thumb. *Good luck, Vitri.* And she means it. She can't do this anymore. She won't. As she turns, she slips the backpack from her shoulders and shoves the pistol in its largest pocket. Facing north, feeling lighter, feeling weightless, she begins upshore at a quick pace, and with long strides, ignoring the pain in her groin and abdomen, digging into the gravel, shoving off with power, with optimism. To what, she isn't certain, but she intends to return to nothing—the rolled Jeep, her dead mother, that home on LaFontaine, fifteen yards, thirty, thinking not of where she'll go, but of what she needs to find, progress immediately stifled by the sight of three masked boys cresting a hill across the river.

Three boys. Northeast. Three boys, all with blue faces and bare torsos, one tall and slender, one shorter and stockier. The last, trailing behind, stands no higher than Reyn's waist. For reasons unclear even to her, she does not run. She does not seek cover. She doesn't even tighten her grip on the pistol. She just stands there, watching as the tallest—carrying what at this distance appears to be a shovel, its edge rusted, its long, crooked handle the same shade as the surrounding branches and bark—no more than forty feet from their side of the river, starts digging a hole. The stocky one stands nearby and swings a white cylindrical pail to and fro, swaying either to something Reyn cannot hear, or something on repeat between his ears. The shortest boy dances—twirls, then hops, then jumps—ceasing only when his blue mask falls off and is swept away by a gust of wind. She watches him chase after it, bend over, pick the mask up with his left hand, place it back over his face and return to a standing position. She watches him notice her. Watches him raise his right arm, the stump she now sees it to be, amputated somewhere near the elbow. Watches him wave at her. Back and forth, back and forth, back-forth, back-forth, until turning to the other boys, who, Reyn sees now, are pointing at the sky. Without so much as one more glance at Reyn, the small boy sprints toward the other boys, once there scooping up two large silver discs the stockier boy isn't able to fit into his pail. Over the hill he goes. Over the hill the other two go, out of Reyn's sight. Only then does she look up.

At first, there is nothing. Clouds, high and swollen. One small bird skimming the western treeline. And then it is there: one large shadow moving over her, over the river, its host a red and yellow plane flying low, flying northeast, a mist spreading from its tail, descending, arcing as the plane does, over the hills, over the trees. It circles southwest, releasing more of its mist as the initial layer reaches the ground, smelling, and tasting, to Reyn like some stale relative of vinegar. As she follows the plane with her eyes, she spots Vitri, sprinting the shoreline, fifty yards from her and closing, a sight that urges her to take off her backpack and dig for the pistol. Vitri slows to a walk. Plugs his fingers into the sky once the pistol is on him. Looks back, looks up, looks at Reyn as the plane approaches once more, and then waves his arms, waves his hands, all toward the western trees. He pulls his scarf down. Waves. Shouts.

"Go!   Run!"

###

Vitri can't hear his voice; he can only feel it, those long strings of sound from throat to armpit, dissipating as Reyn sprints to the woods, as he stops shouting, when it gives way to a chain of coughs. Though he struggles to maintain a straight line, Vitri follows Reyn, the blur she has become. Forward. Forward. Forward, gasping for air between coughs. Forward, until he stumbles beneath trees. Until he is on his knees. On his cheek. Pine needles sticking to his lips. He massages the earth with his fingers. Listens to the plane circle the river. Shuts his eyes.

Vitri wakes on his back. Reyn stands over him with an uncapped water bottle in her hand. As soon as she sees that he is awake, she proceeds to drench his face with what water remains. He sits up, smears the water over his cheeks, spits. He figures he'll try to stand then but, when he sees that Reyn has sat on the ground, feet from him, notebook on her lap, there he stays, wiggling his legs awake, anticipating another swoop from the plane. Hears nothing. Sees nothing.

YOU'RE WEAK

Vitri nods. He nods again when Reyn waves the notebook in front of his eyes. When he reaches for the notebook and pen, she yanks both away.

YOU'RE WEAK

"Yes, I am," Vitri says. He reaches for the notebook and pen once more. She pulls away. Writes hard, writes fast.

IS THERE REALLY A TOWN?

Vitri nods. Convinced he's capable of walking now, he pushes himself off of the ground. But his progress is stymied by Reyn, who rises, who smothers him without making contact. I'M NOT FINISHED, the gesture says. So Vitri sits back down. And, like he'll do when they resume their trek to the town, when Reyn won't be able to stop aiming her eyes east, he is left with the weight of the lies she isn't allowing him to tell: I NEVER INTENDED FOR LAST NIGHT TO HAPPEN. I NEVER WANTED TO HURT YOU. I'M A BETTER PERSON THAN THAT. He'd write that her pointing the .22 pistol at his chest had made him realize that he'd done this before, that he'd driven away someone like her, to anger, to hatred, to a dead end. He rubs his eyes. A lump emerges in the back of his throat and he cannot swallow it.

WE LEAVE ONE ANOTHER AT THE TOWN

Vitri reads. Nods. Rubs his eyes once more. Watches Reyn put away the notebook, the pen, the pistol, then stand, and walk off without looking back.

Pine needles, leaves, and twigs thinning, revealing a sad current trickling. Geese on the eastern shore of the river fling brown water over their necks. The river widens and, together, Reyn and Vitri veer west, following the bend up the gradual slope.

Four buildings populate the west side of the town's lone dirt road. Marked in white paint on rotting plywood, feet above fruit pallets serving as doors, from north to south: McPHERSON's PUB, McPHERSON's HARDWARE, McPHERSON's CLOTHING and McPHERSON's ACCOUNTING, each hodge-podged, constructed with bricks of varying color—dark red here, light blue there, a yellow, a green, an orange, none of the four buildings like the other. Between each building are two-foot-wide alleys cluttered with step-ladders and five-gallon buckets half-filled with what Vitri—drawing closer and closer, hand on his pistol's grip—confirms to be mortar. The road itself, though it dead-ends with cattails and tree stumps twelve feet after McPHERSON's ACCOUNTING, houses nothing but these buildingd. No debris, no gutted vehicles, no bodies, just dirt, the occasional divot from which a boulder has been removed.

Walking alongside the fronts of each building, Vitri passes windows of all shapes and sizes—some tall, skinny and towering, some oddly just smaller than a business envelope, others as long as his hand but as wide as he is tall. All are intact. Smeared, yes, with fingerprints, the sporadic palm, but clear and glared enough by the sun that Vitri has to press his face to the glass to peer in. Barstools of varying heights are scattered throughout the pub, turbulently surrounding the mismatched café tables anterior to a bar of brick-supported plywood. Atop of oak trunk shelves behind the bar are mason jars filled with clear and amber liquids. There is a four-spout tap.

The hardware store has hammers on hooks, cardboard shelves bowing beneath various tool belts, power drills and handsaws. A drill press guards the door.

Inside McPHERSON's CLOTHING are displays of ratty sneakers and boots, dilapidated sandals, pairs of heels here and there. The two mannequins toward the back sport faded ball caps whose brands are illegible. Draped over their necks and shoulders are silk scarves and faux leather belts.

The east side of the road is scant in comparison, one modest brick building appearing lonely but somehow stout, equipped with a thick glass door and accompanying windows to its right and left. McPHERSON's THEATRE, its sign declares and toward its doors walks Reyn. Vitri watches her stop and gawk at the posters hanging in each window. *Citizen Kane. The Man Who Shot Liberty Valance.* Action stills. A black and white Orson Welles gripping a podium. An armed and saturated Jimmy Stewart in contrast. He watches her resume her stride, and though he cannot pinpoint what triggers it, something in Vitri shifts. The whole thing shifts. Replaced is the river with the distant cityscape of Waco. Gone is the gravel; beneath him is asphalt. Beside him is his truck. The theatre is reduced to a one-story schoolhouse, the glass doors of which capture a fogged reflection of his son's curious face. One month ago. The last time the two of them were alone.

"He asks about you," his wife had said the night before, bundling herself in a quilt before lying on her and Vitri's bed, beside their sleeping son. "About where you go."

"What do you tell him?" Vitri asked, situating his makeshift bed on the carpet.

"I tell him what you tell me." She then rolled to her stomach. Laid her cheek on the pillow with no apparent intent to elaborate.

Vitri sat on the foot-end of the bed. He placed his hand on her covered calf. Contemplated telling her what he'd done that day only after she'd yanked her leg away. That, like many other days, he'd driven to the junkyard and, as quietly as he could, switched out the half-filled excrement drums for emptier barrels and five-gallon pails. That, as he scooped out canned peas with his fingers, he watched the sad Brazos flow around a Geo Metro impaled by a sharp edge of a downed log. That at dusk and from a distance he watched a single file line of people enter a church. That within moments the church was aflame. That no one sought exit.

"You can't tell him that I do nothing," Vitri said.

Vitri's wife rolled back over, her eyes barely visible in the dark. "I can't tell him that you do the exact same thing as we do, can I?"

"What do you mean?"

"You wait, Vitri." She said this with an ease that signaled to Vitri that she'd ran the thought through her mind over, and over, and over. "You've never felt more at home, never felt more like Waco was your city than you do now, alone, up on some soapbox you constructed. You say you wait for the world to tilt back to normal. You say you wait for people to return." She rolled back over. "And, if that's true, what you do is exactly what I do, day in, day out; you just do it in a different part of town."

Vitri began tallying the hours he'd spent in thought, the afternoons at Cameron Park, sitting amongst the tall grass and weeds, feet from where he'd proposed to her, the mornings he'd attempt to siphon gas from the same cars on the same streets, in case gallons had magically appeared overnight, how he'd sit on the curb after one or two and feel sorry for himself—

"You don't think I need to be alone sometimes?" His wife asked.

"I got it."

"Huh? Don't you think that'd be nice for me?"

"I said I got it."

He woke his son early the next morning. Staved off his own anxiety as he led his son to the truck and did his best to demonstrate how he wanted him to lay on the floor, tucked out of sight, beneath the glove compartment. Drove to the rural schoolhouse, something Vitri had justified was both new and familiar to the boy. Felt pride in how his son, despite the amount of dust, treated each and every abandoned object with respect—the reams of paper, the books, the calculators, the rulers, the chalkboards. And Vitri felt joy, in how, on the drive home, his son, tucked beneath the glove compartment once more, giggled at each pothole Vitri rumbled over with the S10. And Vitri laughed, and Vitri swerved, and the boy giggled harder, and Vitri laughed harder, and they both seemed to, just for a moment, forget all that had—

Reyn tugs at the doors of the theatre. The locks rattle. The glass jiggles. She tries again, and again, and again, leaning her weight back, back so, so far.

Vitri is forced to re-enter the present. *Stop*, he thinks. *You're being too loud. Stop.* He wills his legs to move. Walks across the road, to her. Fifteen feet away. Ten. Eight.

"Hey!" a voice from behind Vitri. A man's voice but cracking, low to high, bass to tenor. It's a voice that hasn't been stretched this far in some time. "Take your hand off our fucking door!" Footsteps follow the voice, gravel embedding between treads.

Vitri grips the 9mm as he turns, slowing only when he sees that it not just one man, but two, fifteen feet apart and walking toward the theatre, arms outstretched, pistols aimed. One is auburn-bearded and in a loose white tank and blue jeans, the other clean-shaven and wearing camoflauged cargo pants and a black baseball cap. Behind them, the door to McPHERSON's ACCOUNTING is open.

Reyn continues to tug.

"Tell her to stop," black baseball cap says, voice deep, heavy, and smooth, rolling off his tongue with the subtlest of southern drawls.

Vitri reaches out to Reyn. Taps her on the shoulder. She turns around and, upon seeing the two men, juts her arms into the sky. *Two*, Vitri thinks. Two bullets left in the 9mm. Maybe three.

The two men stop in the middle of the road, twenty feet away.

"Toss out the boom stick," the bearded man says. "Toss it on the ground or, we shit you not, we will shoot."

There is no hesitation. Vitri tosses the 9mm to the dirt. Looks at Reyn. Her hands are still in the air. Her eyes are fastened to the ground.

"Smart move," the bearded anm says. Later, Vitri will look at the man's thick head of hair and be reminded of high tide, it looking like some rust-colored wave crashing on his right ear. The tattoos on his shoulders have faded to grey and are crisped over with peeling skin. He keeps his pistol aimed as he closes the gap between he and his counterpart.

The man in the black cap shoves his silver pistol in his hip holster. Approaches Vitri. His eyes are two hazel stones dropped in a still pond, wrinkles rippling down his cheeks. "What color are you?" he asks, grabbing Vitri's scarf. His hand smells of shaving cream. There is a nick along his upper lip seeping red.

"What color?" Vitri asks.

"Yeah, motherfucker, what color are you?" The bearded man presses the barrel of his pistol to Vitri's temple.

"Aggression's the obvious answer, isn't it?" The man takes off his black cap. Squints into the sun. Rubs his hand over his thinning scalp. Puts his hat back on. "Jesus, back off a little, would ya?" he says to the bearded man. "Pick up his gun." Seeing that his partner has obeyed, he then reaches out his hand. "What's in the backpack?"

Vitri slowly slides the backpack from his shoulders. "I carry the weapons," he says. Without looking at Reyn, he adds, "She carries the food."

The man in the black cap unzips Vitri's backpack and inserts his hand. "You're the armory," he says to Vitri, "and she's the diner. That's cute."

Don't take her .22, don't take her .22.

The bearded man shoves Vitri's pistol in his waistband. Stares at Reyn. "Bullshit," he says. Steps toward her. "Give me that fuckin' bag."

"What did I just say?" the man in the black cap says. "Calm. The fuck. Down." He shoves Vitri's toothbrush into the front pocket of his cargo pants, returns the backpack to Vitri, then proceeds to graze his hands over all of Vitri's pockets, the only sound that of paper crumpling. "Just pat her ass down." He finds Vitri's folded knife. Places that into a different pocket. "You heard the man—they ain't masked—so stop being so damn disrespectful."

Crouched to Reyn and ignorant of his partner's shaking head, the bearded man pats down Reyn's shoulders and torso, hips and legs. He points at the bruise on her cheek. "He do that to you, sweetheart?"

"Her name's Jane," Vitri says.

"I asked her, not you," the bearded man says. His smile is ear-to-ear, but crooked, the right side of his face dominant, the left stiff.

"She's a deaf mute," Vitri says.

The bearded man stops. Backs away. Looks at Reyn as if she'd just become a defective toy to be shipped back to its manufacturer.

"Daughter?" the man in the black cap asks.

Vitri nods.

"Who did that to her face?"

"Two masked men."

The man in the black cap nods. Crosses his arms. Anchors his weight to his heels. "Red?"

"Yeah."

"They can do a number," the bearded man says. "Especially to pretty daughters."

"What's your name?" the man in the black cap asks.

"Pete."

"And where are you two headed, Pete?"

"Florida."

The man in the black cap goes to speak, but cannot find the words. He opens his mouth. Two of his teeth have decayed to grey. Closes his mouth without a sound. He turns to the bearded man. "Hear that?"

"I heard 'em." The bearded man spits on the gravel.

"Florida's gone, Pete," the bearded one says. He leans over a map of North America he unfolded seconds ago and set atop the metal desk on the southern side of McPHERSON'S ACCOUNTING. From panhandle to gulf, a large black X signifies the state's demise. The Great Lakes are shaded in. A third of Canada. The northern three-quarters of Mexico. Pockets of the northeastern seaboard.

"Gone?" Vitri says.

Ogden straightens his back. Folds his arms. Shakes his head. "You ever see pictures of the drill they supposedly used to dice up that asteroid?"

Vitri nods. Recalls magazine covers atop grocery store newsstands, video clips of newscasters climbing into a space simulator. Remembers how absurd he thought the panic was, the urgency to buy products that, if an asteroid of that magnitude did hit, the consumers wouldn't be alive to use. Remembers comparing it to the Y2K scare as a teenager; thinks now, albeit briefly, of how much his eyes had aged from one to the next.

"They wheeled that motherfucker in, lined her up at the border and let her rip. Never seen so much goddamn dirt chewed up in my life. Piles of it," Ogden says. "Mountains."

Vitri, flanking the map, looks at Bass, who sits in a leather office chair behind an identical metal desk. "They pulled Florida from the continental United States?" Vitri asks. "Who's they?"

Bass points at Ogden.

Ogden glances at the small tattoo halfway up his forearm, the two ascending jets faded with time and sun, more like ravens than jets at all. "Air National Guard," he says. His voice slips into imitating a superior's orders. "'Gear up. Report to route whatever-the-fuck.' That's all we did: patrol the goddamn roads with our rifles, redirect the curious, send them on their concerned way." He pauses. "We heard the drill, sure— fuckin' thing sounded like a thousand chainsaws—but none of us thought anything of it until we saw those mountains of dirt, until they told us to move to new roads. See, they hauled that shit miles north of the border. Dumped it all. Created some kind of wall. After a while, we didn't hear it anymore. Weren't allowed to leave, though. 'Stay put,' they said. 'Job ain't over.' So we stayed."

Vitri glances at Reyn, who stands alone near the western wall, peering down the narrow hallway that leads south. He watches her gaze at the magazine clippings stapled to the walls. Centerfolds of long-legged brunettes, snippets of petite blondes with perky breasts. She leans down to inspect the three plastic crates on the hardwood floor, one overflowing with canned goods, another with dozens of syringes, some empty, some containing Ohapila. The last crate is home to a pile of assorted masks. Leather, plastic, even metal. Red and yellow, green and blue.

"Martinez was the one that saw the drilling from the air," Ogden says. "Watched its pieces pulled across the gulf. 'Tugboats the size of Connecticut,' he said."

"Martinez was a pilot," Bass says. He swivels in his chair, and panics when he spots a small jar of Vaseline atop the window sill nearest his desk. He swipes the jar, sets in the top drawer of his desk, then nervously fiddles with the loose back of his chair, waiting for something from Vitri, for anything, a nod, a question, a laugh. "You think I can't see 'bullshit' written all over your face, Pete? Think I can't see that you doubt us?"

"I," Vitri starts, throat noosed by the words he hopes can justify his expression, "I just—how long ago did this happen, the drilling?"

Ogden scratches his bearded chin as if it will help him articulate what his memories are whispering. "Eight months, maybe nine. Me and Martinez, well me and Martinez—"

152

"Where is he anyway?" Bass asks. He stands. Adjusts his belt.

"Martinez ain't no sprinting man," Ogden says, annoyed by his counterpart's interruption. "You know that." He adjusts his posture as if he were intending to elaborate upon the story of Florida.

"Well, we can't finish that cellar without him, can we?"

Vitri thinks of the planes. Of manhole clouds. Of cargo. Blankets of chemicals. Doesn't know if it's possible for Ogden, Bass, and this Martinez; doesn't think them capable.

"He'll be back soon, Bass."

Bass, looking out the open front door as if Martinez will suddenly appear, says: "You know we're behind schedule." His tone breaks, from one of relative control to one of anger, of jealousy, of realization that Ogden has had the floor almost since the moment they entered the building, lending an education to their guest, framing himself as the wise one in the room. "One day we're having our shit stolen by those blue fuckers, the next we're—"

"That was one goddamn time," Ogden interrupts.

Bass looks at Vitri. "This bastard," he says, "one day, hmm, a month or two ago, decides it's in our best interest to start trading with those kids—you've seen 'em, right? Boys, blue masks? Four or five of 'em just across the river?"

Vitri shakes his head.

"No shit?" Bass looks at Ogden, who, seeming to know where this is going, leans against the nearest wall and crosses his arms. *Go on with it*, his posture says. *Get it out of your system.* "Well, one day, when me and Martinez are gone lugging gas God knows where, all of 'em come here." He points past Reyn, at the narrow hallway. "Because Ogden's lazy ass is napping in the back room, they startle him when they pound on the door. Boosh-boosh, boosh-boosh, boosh-boosh. And Ogden, as he tells it, says he got up, rifle in hand, ready to blast whoever the fuck was there. But when he opens the door, there they are, carrots in hand. Radishes. Goddamn broccoli."

Vitri nods, though he, having not heard a person verbally go to these lengths since Hammer, processes little. *Slow the fuck down*, he thinks, overwhelmed by the voices,

153

the words, the rapidity, the rambling, the conjuring of pointless memories. Wonders what it is that drives a person to open up to a stranger, whether it's a desire to fill the silence, or if they think the awkwardness of exposed isolation can be hidden behind mounds of words. Because he can see loneliness in both Ogden and Bass. He can hear it. They've heard these words before; they've spoken these words before; these words are at once what keeps them feeling lonely and what makes them feel loved.

"And Ogden sees no problem with it. Thinks, 'Hmm, those veggies look pretty damn tasty,' and, I mean, I can't fault him for that. Not at all. They *were* good. But as Ogden's doing all this, as he's handing the kids some chunks of wood, some nails, whatever, the tiniest bastard's across the street, climbing in and out of the goddamn theatre and—"

"—Stealing reels," Ogden interjects.

"So," Bass continues, annoyed, "It takes five minutes or so for Ogden to realize it's going on at all. When he does, off go the three that were standing in front of him, just bounding down the shore there, tiptoeing across the river on that clay support we spent three weeks building."

"I got his ass though, didn't I?" Ogden says to Bass. He looks at Vitri. "Snatched up the little fucker, brought him back here."

"Took his arm." Bass straightens his right arm and motions his left hand as if it were a cleaver, slicing where ulna meets radius. "He won't be stealing again."

Vitri looks at Reyn. Wishes she'd stop touching those masks, twirling those cans. Silence.

"He died then, the boy?" Vitri asks. He feels like he is at the store again, behind the counter, letting customers talk, stoking their conversational fire with disingenuous questions he doesn't need the answer to.

"I see him every now and then," Ogden says. "He just does his own thing, really. All of them do. Wander around, dig their holes—"

"These ones aren't at all like the savages that did that number to her face," Bass says. "Savages," Ogden says. "That's what those reds are. Fucking savages."

"Goddamn savages," Bass says.

Silence.

"Us? We were posted at rural airstrips. Sometimes regional airports," Ogden says from behind the MᴄPHERSON's PUB bar. He carries over two mason jars—one of dark beer, one of light—and sets them in front of Reyn and Vitri. "Marines and SEALs locked down the internationals."

"Thank you," Vitri says to Bass. Then, to Ogden: "Why there?"

Ogden steps back behind the bar and grabs two shot glasses and a bottle of bourbon.

"Sounds like you were one of the smart ones and stayed home," Bass says, "but, for the first few weeks of the blackout, wave after wave of people were in search of planes. They assumed they could barter for a flight, that, with as little as a few soon-to-be-worthless dollars, they'd be able to bribe some stubborn pilot into taking them out of the country." After Ogden sits down, Bass grabs the bottle of bourbon and pours himself a shot. Downs it. "And, well, there Ogden would be."

"Orders were simple: protect the planes." Ogden follows suit, takes a shot. "If people drove up, were civil in asking us questions, we'd tell them to fuck off and go on their merry way. And they would. Nobody really put up a fight. But if they came in numbers, if they approached aggressively, orders were to neutralize."

"And if they somehow broke through the lines," Bass says, "if they reached an aircraft with someone competent enough to fly the damn thing, that's where Martinez would come in."

"He'd circle all day. Make his rounds. Refuel. Make his rounds, refuel."

Vitri sips the dark beer. Frothy, homemade, bitter. Pictures Carmen at sea, treading water after leaping from the edge of a floating landmass, somehow escaping the state before the drilling. Clinging to the hope of self-brought closure. He nudges the other mason jar toward Reyn, attempting to understand how difficult this must be like for her, watching the three of them without say, waiting without say, following commands and cues without say—drink this, look at this, come this way. *The world's subordinate*. "Did you ever—?"

"Kill anyone?" Ogden says. He pours another shot. "No. Like I said, people were pretty civil about it all. Then again, word spreads, you know? People tend to wise up once they see or hear one or two go down."

"None of this happened in—" Bass pauses. "Where are you two from?"

Vitri looks at Reyn. She sniffs her beer, rotates her glass. Sniffs it some more. "San Antonio."

"Nothing of the sort there?"

"If there was, we didn't see it. Certainly didn't see anyone digging up any border."

"It'll happen," Bass says. He downs another shot. "You just wait. It'll happen. Louisiana's next and I assume they'll just keep working their way west, treating the land like it's a fucking jigsaw puzzle." He pours more bourbon.

Ogden starts laughing, but not at Bass. "First drink with the old man?" he says, referring to Reyn's scrunched face.

Vitri forces a smile, though it pains him to see how hard Reyn is trying to keep the beer in her mouth. "This is a first, that's for sure."

"How old is young Jane anyway?" Ogden asks.

Vitri doesn't know. Doesn't want to consider it yet again. "Sixteen," he says for his own benefit, then looks down at the table. Sips his beer.

"Only kid?"

Vitri nods.

"And deaf to boot?"

Vitri nods.

"Jesus," Ogden says. "Got yourself a pretty little wife though, I suppose?"

Fuck you. "I did, yeah," Vitri says. He stares into the mason jar. Pictures her lying in that shallow hole, entry wound just above her ear. Hair stained red, coyotes' teeth stained red, all stained red.

"How'd she go?" Bass asks.

Vitri fidgets in his chair. Scratches his neck. *Suicide.* Announces as honestly as he can, "Savages."

"Savages," Ogden says.

"Savages," Bass says.

They all take a drink. Even Reyn.

Silence.

Vitri watches Ogden lift his right arm and scratch his armpit. Inches beneath the clump of auburn-colored hair are small groupings of scars, all pink and no wider than a pen's point. He clears his throat. "This is great, guys. Really, thank you," he says. He watches Ogden and Bass nod their responses. "I think that what you guys have done here—these buildings—it's all beautiful, beautiful work. I guess what I'm not understanding is, well, I imagine all of this has taken a long time. Gathering the materials, raising the walls with only three men—"

"Gonna be a while before we get it just right, too," Bass says. "River has to dry up a bit more but, when it does, we're heading north. We're heading east. We're expanding."

"Bridges," Ogden says. "Gazebos."

"Have us some plans for a restaurant, a grocery store, even a hotel." Bass doesn't bother pouring himself another shot. Swigs from the bottle instead. "I'm being rude, though. I cut you off, and I apologize." Bass doesn't bother to look at Ogden. *Ask me*, his stare says. *Ask me*. "Please continue, Pete."

"Why?" Vitri says. "Why do it?"

Despite his low, heavy voice, Bass's cackle is piercing.

Ogden has no reaction.

"I'm sorry," Bass says. "I do intend to answer you. But first," he says, leaning forward, "do you mind if I ask you a few questions?"

After sipping from his beer, Vitri works to mirror Bass: shoulders hunched, leaning forward. "Sure."

"Just looking at you," Bass says, "my guess would be that you're somewhere in your thirties. Upper thirties, mid-to-upper. But how old are you?"

"Forty-two."

"And what was it you did before this lovely nation of ours turned to shit? Did you sit in a cubicle and crunch numbers, populate the fuck out of a spreadsheet? Were

157

you posting links all day and interacting with commenters? Did you barf some shit on a blank blog page and watch the clicks pile up?"

"I owned and operated a store."

"What kind of store?" Bass asks, eyes narrowed, upset at being off in his assessment. When Vitri points to the scarf on his neck, Bass smiles. "Still sporting your own brand, huh? Now that's dedication." He raises his shot glass to Ogden, though Ogden pays little attention, eyes flickering at Reyn every few seconds. "You build the store from the ground up then?"

Vitri shakes his head. "Parents did. Passed it down to me when they'd had enough."

"Sounds about right," Bass says. His tone says he has rediscovered comfort, a comfort that comes only with being right. "See, and my guess is that you had yourself a small staff, if any staff at all, and that, by the end of the day, by closing time, you, exhausted Pete, were ready to tap out, to throw in the towel. You were ready to have that fucking store demolished, am I right? I mean, just how much time were you able to devote to little Jane over there? An hour on Sundays? Maybe two?"

"Still wish I'd had more," Vitri says.

"And how about your pretty wife? How many times you fuck her each week?"

Silence.

"Never enough, right?" Bass takes another swig from the bottle. "And that's my point. Don't go feeling bad about it, because that was me, too." Another swig. "See, for nine years I worked construction. Had this shit boss named Thompson that paid me what he deemed I was worth to tweak strip malls, to build China Woks and Red Woks and Blue Woks and any kind of fucking Wok you can think of."

Vitri notices Bass's hands then, dirt-crusted calluses along each palm, a festered blood blister on the stretch of skin between his right thumb and index finger, a large grey oval needing only a pin prick to burst red.

"By year nine, I was pretty damn good. Had lived beneath that line they call poverty all my life so I appreciated my raises, the one-percents and the two-percents, the small handouts that keep the desperate coming back. Still enjoyed some aspects of the job, too. Enough not to tell Thompson to fuck off and quit, at least. Well, one day, I get one of these handouts. Unexpectedly, no less. Just some Tuesday or Wednesday, Thompson drives out to the strip mall me and my crew are at, finds me, and says, 'You can cut out early today. You deserve it.' And, you know what? I did deserve it. I took that money, I got in my truck and I went home, thinking that, hey, tonight we'll celebrate a bit. I'll take my wife and boys out to dinner and a movie. Didn't even matter where we ate, or what we saw. Didn't make the slightest of fucking differences to me." Bass takes a deep breath. "So I go home, to the two-bed-two-bath we could afford, and what do you think I find when I get there?" Bass pauses. Refuses to blink. "I walk in and I see two men fucking my wife. Right there, on the living room sofa. And I go numb. I mean, I can't-even-shut-the-door-behind-me numb. I just watch. But then, to my left, I hear a voice—I hear my youngest whisper, 'Daddy.' So I look, and there, beside him, is his brother. Both are just standing in the hallway, watching. So I go ballistic. I take the ball-point hammer from my tool belt and beam one of the guys in the back of the head. The other one pulls out of my wife and proceeds to beat the hell out of me. In front of my cheating wife, in front of my sons, still hard, boner swinging all over the damn place." Bass's stare becomes distant, the memory still vivid, the wound still open.

"I'm really sorry to hear that," Vitri says.

Bass waves off Vitri's apology. "No need. Past is the past, right?" He leans in. "That doesn't mean that I didn't spend months trying to find the why. That's what we do, isn't it, try to find the why? Even if it isn't there, that's what we look for, omitting the when, the what and the how. Pointless. Dog chasing their tail kind of shit. But, with my wife, there was a why. There was a reason why she did what she did. There was a reason why she won custody. There was a reason why she moved to Missouri." Bass pauses. "The reason is routine."

"Routine?"

"Routine," Ogden says.

"My routine," Bass says. "For nine years, I'd be up and gone by six to some job site, never to be seen by or heard from until seven, even eight on some nights. Did I have to do that? Did I have to work those hours? No. Hell no. I could've shortened it

159

by at least a few, told her to find some work, enrolled the boys in a day care. But did I? Nope. I wanted her to watch the kids. I wanted to be the bread-winner. I wanted to be the lone supporter of the family. All that old-timey pride shit. Blah fucking blah." Another swig from the bottle. "So what was she supposed to do? Cook all damn day? Call her friends while they were at work? No. Not a chance. Took me a while to realize that. Took getting fired. Took telling my lawyer I couldn't afford him. Took several hours spent alone. But, when I did, I started my own business. Worked whenever I wanted to, whenever I needed to, whenever I felt like it. World started going under. Saw an opportunity so I called Ogden."

"Came here as soon as I could," Ogden says.

"Yes, yes, you did," Bass says. He punctuates his gratitude with a swig from the bottle, which, between the two of them, is half-gone.

Unlike before, Vitri is not lost in this conversation. He just doesn't know what to say. He watches Bass's hand briefly. How he bounces his index and middle fingers on the table makes it seem that he is craving a cigarette.

"I'll tell you what, though," Bass says to Vitri, "that whole thing, that whole fucking mess made me a better person. You want to know why? You want to know *that* why? Huh, Pete, do you?" When Vitri still utters nothing, Bass leans in closer. "The how's important here. Ask me how."

Vitri makes it a point to not let Bass's abrasiveness linger. Says immediately: "How did it make you a better person?"

"It taught me just how malleable we are. Torqued to fit some scheme a fucker thought up from his gravestone, until we don't know how to take a step back and examine the big picture, until we blindly accept that mediocrity." Bass leans back. Crosses his arms. "We're resistant only when our routines are challenged. Which makes for quite the cluster fuck in a time of crisis. 'The world's gone to shit,' we say, looking back fondly on those long ass drives to work, that shitty gas station coffee we sipped. But, really, so fucking what if the world's gone to shit? So fucking what?" Bass takes one last sip from the bottle of bourbon, then plugs the opening with its stray cork. "It doesn't for one second mean that your life wasn't already shit. Know what I'm saying?"

I don't. "I do," Vitri says, eyes on the cork, hoping it means that this will soon be over, that in moments Bass will rise from the table, then Ogden, and send he and Reyn on their way. "I really do."

"I'm glad you do," Bass says. "But I apologize."

"For what?"

"I don't believe I've given a proper answer to your question. You asked me why, why we're doing this, you asked what the fucking point was. And though I can only speak for myself here, the answer is quite simple: as an assimilating man of a confused society, I inadvertently forced everything I loved out of my life. My home, my wife, my children, everything just gone. Like snow in June." Bass leans forward. "But you know what? Turn the world upside-down and you give the wounded man an opportunity to build precisely what he wants. So fuck it, pull us out to sea, sell us to goddamn Spain, or Sweden, or Japan, whatever the fuck country. *This* is what I'll have when we're pulled through the waves."

Silence.

Vitri looks from Bass to his beer, from his beer to Reyn, who stares at the ceiling.

"Boy should've run for mayor," Ogden says.

Ogden locks the pub after Vitri, Reyn and Bass walk out to the road. The sky is clear, the sun high, looping toward night. Bass leads them all toward McPHERSON'S ACCOUNTING once more, where Reyn and Vitri's few belongings remain.

"If I were you two," Bass begins, without turning to acknowledge them, "I'd turn right around. Head northwest. They say Seattle hasn't been touched yet."

"Seattle? Really?" *Not going to Seattle.* Not for a second. *Not going west.* Whether Reyn comes along or not, he'll walk north, if only to allow Ogden and Bass to believe they'd made an impact, and then he'll turn east. Somehow, he'll cross the river, and, somehow, he'll cross into Florida, and, somehow, he'll find Carmen. He'll do it. Over an hour of wasted words won't alter his aim.

"Really," Bass says, then stops. Turns around. "You two go on ahead. We'll be right there." He steps to the side and waves Reyn and Vitri off.

161

Which strikes Vitri as odd only after they have passed, when he looks back to see Ogden and Bass, halted, and whispering, words unintelligible from a dozen feet away. Vitri stops. Reyn continues, looks back at Vitri once she reaches the McPHERSON'S ACCOUNTING door.

More whispers.

As politely as he can, Vitri clears his throat, then says, "Guys, I think we're hoping to cover some ground before sundown."

More whispers. More. And then Ogden and Bass resume walking.

"I just think she's getting a little antsy is all," Vitri says. "Ready to move."

"I don't think Jane looks antsy at all," Ogden says, continuing toward Reyn.

"Before you two do take off," Bass says, "me and Ogden here have a proposal."

Vitri's mind jolts from one possibility to the next, from Bass asking he and Reyn to stay and run one of the stores, to Bass enlisting their help for the construction of that gazebo.

"What would that be?" Vitri asks.

Ogden steps closer to Reyn; Bass steps closer to Vitri.

"It's important to note, Pete," Bass says, "that what we want from you is going to happen whether you accept the proposal or not. The reason we're proposing anything is, well, we were just talking, and you seem like a good man, Pete, a smart man, a man who understands trade." When all Bass receives from Vitri is a squint, he continues, "What I mean to say is that, despite all that's happened to this here land, Ogden and I still believe that there's a time and a place that civility must be maintained. And this is just such a time. We believe that a father's consent is important."

"Bottom line is that neither me or Bass here have been able to take our eyes off your daughter. Bruises and all, I'd bet she's the best piece of pussy to come through here."

"Pardon Ogden's language," Bass says, "but he's right. As offensive as he may be, he's right." Bass glares at Ogden. "Women just don't come through here very often."

"And when they do, they're always two days from death," Ogden says.

162

Bass looks to Ogden. "You're making a goddamn fool of yourself." He returns his eyes to Vitri. "It's also important for you to know, Pete, that we have no intentions of harming your daughter. There will be no violence. You will find no new bruises on her body. You have my word."

Silence.

Vitri stares at Bass. Shifts from Bass to Reyn, from Reyn to Ogden. Back to Reyn.

"What do you say, Pete?" Bass circles. Places himself between Vitri and Reyn.

Silence.

Ogden sighs. "Come on," he says beneath his breath.

"You won't hurt her?" Vitri asks.

"We won't hurt her."

Vitri crosses his arms. "And what did you say about trade?"

"Jesus Christ," Ogden says.

"It's his fucking daughter," Bass says. "It takes time to accept such a thing."

"Well if he'd been bending his cousin over a goddamn office chair for months, I'm sure he'd be a little anxious too."

Fury consumes Bass's body. His eyes widen as he steps toward Ogden and swings with a closed right fist. Strikes him in the throat with enough force to send him to the ground, his gasps for air are obstructed by two quick strikes to his chest. Bass pushes himself off of the ground. Stares at a frightened Reyn. Turns to Vitri.

"Trade, yeah, trade," Bass says. Ogden's gasping quiets. He rolls to his side and pushes himself to his feet. "We can do that. Food, weapons, you name it. Name your price."

Vitri looks at Reyn. "What kinds of weapons?"

"Would you rather have a sharp point? Or are you looking for some kick?"

"Rifles?"

Holding his throat, Ogden nods.

"Available for trade?" Bass says. "Three. Two M4s, one Springfield."

"I'll take the two M4s," Vitri says. "And ammo. Enough for Seattle."

Bass turns to Ogden. They nod at one another. "Deal," Ogden struggles to say. He extends a hand, which is not met by Vitri.

"One other condition," Vitri says.

Bass retracts his hand. "What's that?"

"I get to watch." Vitri waits for the confusion to take shape in both of their faces. "You gave me your word that she wouldn't be hurt. But I don't believe you. Not for a fucking second. I need to see it for myself."

"You don't want to watch, Pete," Bass says.

"No matter what, it'll be painful for you," Ogden struggles to say.

"You don't think I've endured pain?"

"Didn't say that," Bass says. He pulls the pistol from his holster. "Didn't say that at all. What I'm saying is that you're not going to watch. You're not going to step foot in that fucking building. You're going to stand out here, we're going to lock that door, and you're going to wait until we're done." Bass steps toward Reyn. "Is that clear?"

Vitri remains still. "Then bring our stuff out here."

"What?"

"Bring our fucking stuff out here then," Vitri says. "If I can't come in, if I can't be by her side, I at least have to tell her—write to her—what's going on. Because right now she has no fucking idea. And she's going to fight. I can promise you that. Unless you allow me to tell her, she's going to bite, and she's going to dig, and she's going to claw."

Ogden and Bass share a look that reveals their skepticism, of Vitri's words, of Reyn's resolve.

"Just fucking get it."

Silence.

Stares.

Unsure footsteps.

"You searched hers, right?"

Ogden nods. "Yes, Bass, yes I did."

You didn't.

"You're sure?"

"Yes," Ogden says.

At that, Bass steps past Reyn and enters the building alone, footsteps creaking across the hardwood. "Go get their shit then," he says.

Ogden follows.

Vitri walks to Reyn. Does not crouch. Can barely look at her.

When Ogden emerges once more from the building, he is shirtless. A thin tribal tattoo wraps from oblique to oblique. The rest is partitioned off by tan-lines, bare and white. In his hand is Reyn's backpack.

"Hurry up," he says as he hands their backpacks over. "You'll get your weapons back when we're through."

Vitri drops the backpacks to the ground, then unzips the largest pocket of Reyn's. He quickly pulls out the notebook and a pen. Zips the pocket shut. Uncaps the pen. Writes. Caps the pen, shoves it into his pocket. *Not up for discussion.* Hands the notebook to Reyn.

GO. TRUST ME

She only reads it once. And, as if she'd been expecting it, as if she knew all along that this exact scenario was going to happen, Reyn, without so much as a glance at Vitri, drops the notebook and leads Ogden into McPHERSON's ACCOUNTING.

"That's a good girl," Ogden says. He shuts the door behind him. Locks it.

Vitri crouches to grab the notebook. Because he knows Bass is watching him from the window, he places it into the backpack as slowly as possible, as dramatically as possible. He looks to the sky as if answers are to be found there. He waits. *Close your eyes, Reyn. It'll be over soon. Just close your eyes.* And he listens.

"You take her clothes off," he hears Bass say.

Ogden: "I get to go first then."

A belt buckle clangs off of the hardwood floor.

"Like hell you do."

"Why wouldn't I?"

Boots are taken off, flung toward a wall.

"Because you told that shithead out there that you fuck me in the ass, that's why."

At that, Vitri re-ties the scarf around his nose and mouth, then reaches back into Reyn's backpack. Finds the sickle. Sets it aside.

VIII.

Over Reyn's lifted arms goes her sweatshirt. Once off, the bearded man folds it gently and sets it on the green-quilted cot to his left. The other man stands nearer to the hallway, naked, watching, working to get his penis hard. His mouth moves but, in this dim light, Reyn cannot pinpoint any particular shapes, any syllables. The bearded man steps back toward her, grinning. He unbuttons her jeans. His fingers find her zipper. They find her belt loops. And—

The floor quivers.

Again.

And again.

The bearded man's fingers stop. He turns his head. The naked man bends to his discarded clothes, locates his pistol, and, with it in his hand, walks down the hallway.

And then the floor is sent into mild convulsions, short but rapid waves striking Reyn's toes.

The bearded man turns away from Reyn entirely. Flash. Flash-flash. Reyn watches the bearded man reach for the pistol on his hip. Flash-flash.

She drops to the floor. Shields her face. Coils her body.

Blood splatters onto her shoulders and back.

Footsteps. More. More.

Reyn unshields her face. The bearded man squirms on the floor, jaws clenched, right shoulder slimed red. She watches Vitri shove the barrel of the pistol she carried into the man's mouth. There it stays for three seconds, four, five, the bearded man trying to speak around the barrel. And then Vitri pulls the trigger. Again, and again, and again. Blood, so much blood, splattered, leaking, pooling around the bits of pulp on the floor. Ears remain, a sliver of an eye.

Vitri stands. Walks down the hallway. Comes back dragging the naked man by his feet. Swivels him next to the bearded man. He lets him speak, then aims the pistol at the man's head and fires, fires, fires, fires until the pistol just won't anymore. Only then does he drop the pistol and walk to Reyn, not once looking her in the eye, not once seeming to notice just how frantically she attempts retreat. Closer now, and closer. He reaches for her. She swats at his arms as he stands her up and reaches for her groin, stopping when, after he buttons her button and zips her zipper, it's clear that Vitri doesn't want her in this moment. She watches him search the underbelly of each cot. Watches him yank a rifle from beneath the one nearest the door—black, compact, and with too many contours for Reyn to count. He checks and rechecks its magazine as he rises and walks down the narrow hallway. Where the hallway meets the front room of McPHERSON's ACCOUNTING, Vitri kneels. Props himself against the wall. Aims the rifle at what Reyn, still in the bedroom, assumes to be the front door.

For minutes he kneels there. For minutes she waits for him to stand once more, approach her once more, write to her once more, explain this, explain it all. For minutes she contemplates bolting. Past him, through him, through a window. She takes a step forward. She takes another—

Three flashes from the rifle.

Vitri stands and walks out of Reyn's sight. She waits a moment before continuing down that hallway. When she does, she is met by Vitri, hunched over, walking backward. Reyn narrows herself against the hallway wall, allowing Vitri the room he needs to drag the Hispanic man dressed neck to toe in black. The Hispanic man's limp right hand skids over Reyn's foot.

Night arrives. The McPHERSON's ACCOUNTING door is still open, the only light for miles the candle upon the desk, its almond scent combating the smell of urine and feces drifting down the hallway. Reyn keeps the candle close, as close as she can. Her fingers are trembling less now, adrenaline slinking somewhere other than her eyes as she watches the flame. Alongside the candle, atop the map, is the notebook, open to a blank page, an uncapped pen propped on its binding. SORRY, she has considered writing. SORRY. Yet, in the time she has been waiting for Vitri to emerge from the bedroom, she has been unable to bring herself to do so, her heart sending the tiniest of jolts to her hand before pen can reach paper. *No*, she thinks it says. And she has been listening. She has been thinking. Letting it churn. *You did not cause this.*

Moments later, when she carries the candle down the hallway, Reyn finds Vitri naked on the floor, his pale skin looking like wax paper in the dim light. He has stacked the three dead men in the northwest corner of the bedroom. He lies on his side, facing the opposite wall. Two empty syringes lie near his hand; two full syringes lie closer to his hip. A small pile of feces is on the floor, some of it clinging to the hair against the backs of his thighs. A puddle of urine expands before his groin.

This is as close as she gets. This is as close as she wants to be. She does not want to see his face. She wants nothing to do with his eyes, wants nothing to do with his hands. She wants nothing of him.

Reyn sets Ralph's sickle on the desk and, next to it, DEEP THROAT. *No weapons.* In their stead, she places more cans of food in her backpack from the plastic crate against the wall. Barley soup, stringed green beans, fiesta corn, spinach. Quickly, Reyn searches Vitri's backpack for anything useful, extracting from it three more palm-sized candles, the flashlight, two and a half bottles of water, and all but one book of matches, which she shoves into her pants pocket. Into her backpack all of it goes, toppling, gravity and shape delegating where it is they'll all rest. Because Reyn is leaving.

She is leaving.

Going, gone.

Far away from here.

Not tonight, though, not in the dark. Doing so, she thinks, would be suicide. Mauled by some starved predator. Crossing paths with yet another man or woman she'll inevitably fail to understand. Cornered into something just like this, just as painful.

Instead, she's going to the theatre. She zips the largest pocket of her backpack, then struggles to slide its straps over her shoulders, the added weight enough to alter her posture. Lifts the lit candle from the desk, then exits, leaving the McPHERSON's ACCOUNTING door open.

Once across the road, she carefully sets the backpack on the ground and, candle in hand, walks to the northern side of the building. Nothing but dirt, and weeds, not even a rock. On the southern side, however, sits a small pile of loose yellow bricks, two of which Reyn grabs with her free hand. Back at the theatre entrance, Reyn sets the candle next to her backpack. She then positions herself just so—feet from the glass door, enough room between for her arm to wind up and follow through, for each brick to gain velocity and make a dent—and, attempting to channel as much anger as she can, throws the first brick. Though a beetle-sized shard of glass has chipped off, she has missed the mark; all she wants, all she needs, is a hole above the handle, large enough to snake her arm through and turn the lock.

Gone, gone, gone, she is gone, they are gone, all are gone and crack-crack, crack-crack, *the sound of glass, the sound of anger, the sound of hope separating, falling where it belongs, where it starts, where it leads, and* crack-crack, crack-crack, crack-crack, crack-crack. Crack-crack—

Gone, all gone—

crack-crack—

you are not floating—

crack-crack—

there is no song—

crack-crack—

you are what makes it end.

When the crack-crack from across the road subsides, Vitri opens his eyes. Beneath the cot nearest him is a boy's head. No body to speak of; just his head, parallel to Vitri's, eyes aligned. Seven years old. Eight. Grey face. Dark, disheveled hair. Violet eyelids. An indifferent stare.

"You did this," the boy says. It is not a whisper. It is not a scream. It is not his son.

"I did," Vitri says. He scoots himself closer to the boy. Wants to feel his cheek. Wants to find the rest of him and hold him close.

A rifle inches itself from under the cot.

"You don't belong here," the boy says.

Vitri stops. Stares at the rifle. "No," he says. He grips the rifle. "No."

And then, like everyone else, the boy is gone. *Gone, gone, gone.*

Once Vitri discontinues his search for the boy, he, rifle in hand, rolls onto his back. Syringes fracture beneath his weight. The pile of feces flattens across the back of his right thigh. He checks the safety. Off. Flips the barrel of the rifle to his chin. Rests the stock on his abdomen. Locates the trigger. Works the barrel of the rifle to the roof of his mouth.

One flash of yellow-white light rushes through MCPHERSON'S ACCOUNTING and spills onto the road, onto Reyn's back.

By the time Reyn can fit her arm through the hole that she has carved in the theatre's glass door, the candle has gone out. Her forehead is damp with sweat. Her breath is heavy. After allowing herself a moment of rest, she reaches her hand through the hole—jagged glass wide enough for her to angle her wrist without being gashed—finds the deadbolt and unlocks the door. She retracts her hand carefully, returns to her backpack and slings it over her shoulders. Then, propping the door open with her hip, she pulls the book of matches from her pants pocket. Re-lights the candle. Enters the theatre.

Half of the floor is carpeted with what Reyn can see now are chunks of various rugs and floor mats, spliced together. A mosaic of sorts. The other half is gravel, atop of which dozens of posters lie, rolled tight and rubber-banded. Near the eastern wall, one projection screen hangs from the rafters. No more than ten feet from the screen sits one row of four bucket seats. Black and grey, beige and red, one cloth, two leather, the last some ratty version of suede, all with gouges mended by duct tape, armrests made of plywood, then partially-wrapped in rubber tubing. Three of the four still have seatbelts, male and female ends dangling.

In the northeastern corner, at the edge of her candle's glow, Reyn spots the lip of a basement staircase. She sets her backpack on one of the chairs facing the projection screen. Carefully places the lit candle on the floor and reaches into her backpack for another. Lights it; waits for the flame to settle. Then, she descends the staircase.

Ten feet down she goes, candlelight gnawing itself up and across the nearest concrete wall. She turns right when she reaches the bottom. Dozens of weapons hug the eastern wall. A pile of pistols. Leaned rifles and shotguns. Further south are two stacks of empty duffel bags, ammunition boxes and cleaning kits between that give the towers structure. Reyn examines little here. Has no interest in utilizing this room's initial offering. It's when she turns to leave that she sees anything of interest: at the edge of her candle's light, in the southwestern corner, lies what she knows to be a generator, its tires dusty, stones lodged between treads. She approaches. Crouches. Hovers the candle over CHOKE, over START, over the small engine and the pull cord. She wonders what would illuminate if she were to start it, wonders what of this town would draw its power from this stout rectangle. She pictures lampposts that have yet to be erected, neon signs that have yet to be placed. She pictures building interiors aglow, the theatre's projector flickering. She pictures wanderers along the river's shore, spooked at the sight but unable to resist their desire to approach, drawn to light like moths. She stands. Assesses. Knows that she won't be able to get it up the stairs by herself, knows but thinks she'll try in the morning anyway, though to what end she is unsure of, finding it hard to picture herself lugging the generator anywhere outside of the town. Upriver. To Monroe. To Idaho.

Back up the stairs she goes. She blows out the candle in her hand. Lets the candle on the floor burn. She sits down, facing the projection screen, knowing that nothing will play, knowing that no one will join her. And, for now, she is more than okay with that. She is content, alone in this theatre, thinking not of Vitri, not of her father, not of Faye, nor her mother, but of herself and of that shipwreck, of the *American Queen*. The size of it. The idea of it being on the river, operational, passengers at the railing, watching the paddlewheel as if it had just been invented. Reyn pictures herself aboard. Before swigging from that open bottle of water and spooning chunks of soup from that pre-opened can at the bottom of her backpack, she wonders if there is a way in, a way to the boat's deck, a ladder or rope to climb, a window to fracture and crawl through. *There has to be.* She pictures herself standing upright in a room forever sideways, taking days to tailor it all to her liking—muscling over the tipped beds, the end tables, the nightstands. She'll read every page, every last word of the books that have flown from the library's shelves, scribbling notes in the margins, observations aligning with what she sees the world as. *At dawn*, she thinks. At dawn she'll start. She'll re-hang the curtains. She'll scrape the sap from whichever healthy trees remain and use it to glue the shattered lamps together. She'll come back here when she's done. Grab the generator. Wheel it north. She'll light what she can.

###

Reyn is at her home on LaFontaine, lying on the living room sofa, and she feels fine. Her cheek has returned to normal, as has her tongue. Nothing of her body throbs. And yet, something feels off to her. Not her body. The home.

Though she for the life of her can't remember what images were seconds before flashing across the television, gone is the picture, reduced to black and white lines whipping like downed electrical wires. She sits up. Blood dribbles down her chin.

The wall nearest the kitchen vanishes, is ripped off like a scab. And through the new opening walks her mother. Her healthy mother. Back is her style. Back is her midsection. Back is her smile. And she walks straight to Reyn. Instructs her to lie her head back. And Reyn does. Feels her mother's fingers caress her throat. Seconds later, her mother stands, turns, walks off.

Reyn sits up. More blood dribbles down her chin. She wipes it away. More spills from her lip. She wipes it away. And there goes the wall nearest her. In walks her father, who, drunk, stumbles toward the kitchen, doing a double-take once he sees Reyn on the couch. He stops. Smiles. Stumbles toward her. Leans down, goes to kiss Reyn on the cheek, stubbled face smearing across her chin. He smiles as he rises, Reyn's blood on his lips.

After him walks Faye. Through the house she goes. Crossing her path is JOHN. Crossing JOHN's path is the old woman with the *American Queen* shirt. Through the house they all go, past Reyn. Oblivious.

Reyn sits up once more. Blood pours from her mouth, down her chin, to her chest, on her lap. She stands but immediately feels weight on her shoulders, a force pressing down-down-down that she fights. And then there are hands, and then there are feet, and then there are shins, and thighs. A chest. Shoulders mirroring hers. She looks up to see Vitri, eyes wide, scarf over his mouth and nose. He shoves her to the sofa. Pins her hands to the cushion. Mounts her. Thrusts. And thrusts. And thrusts, paying no mind to the same people that pass through the house once more—Reyn's mother, Reyn's father, Faye, JOHN, the old woman. Only when he is finished, only when he is face down on Reyn's chest does the roof cave.

Reyn does not wake at dawn, but hours after, when sunlight leaks through the glass and onto the floor. When she does wake, she rises from the two seats she'd shoved together in the night and rubs sleep from her eyes as she walks toward the entrance. It isn't until she begins pushing the door open that she sees the small boy standing in the doorway of McPHERSON's ACCOUNTING, blue mask on and loosely over all but his lips and eyes, the diamond-shaped holes for each glared by sunlight skimming off the plastic. He wears no shirt, only baggy blue shorts that flare at the calf. In his only hand he holds tight the two blue masks he'd found in the crate.

They stand like this, staring at one another across the road. For two seconds, for three seconds, four, and up to eight before Reyn, assuming the boy to not be acting on his own, glances south. As she does so, as she shifts her eyes for but a moment, the small boy takes off. Sprints north, shoulders pumping but head still, legs churning, sandaled feet sending plumes of dust into the sky. Reyn hurries through the doorway and onto the dirt road, scuffing shards of glass along. Before the boy reaches the slope she and Vitri surmounted en route to the town, Reyn sees one of the two masks slip from his grasp and fall to the ground. But soon he is down the hill, out of sight.

Reyn walks north but soon finds herself picking up speed. *He'd come so far,* she thinks, somewhere between a jog and sprint now, feeling the aluminum cans smacking her back. She feels the remaining liquid in the bottle of rubbing alcohol slosh around, jostling for position with the candles.

Reyn struggles over her wounds to bend down and pick up the abandoned mask. But she does and, mask in hand, she covers the remaining yards to the crest of the hill. Looking down on the river, she sees the boy, two hundred yards north, veer slightly to the west, toward the shore's treeline. To the east of him is the river, its coverage growing thicker the further north he goes, its top layer comprised of still-green grass and weeds not yet yellowed by the sun. She focuses on the boy once more, who has begun turning his hips toward the river, his eyes, his feet following, all churning just as fast as before. *Kingfisher.* At this moment, maybe more than ever, Reyn wishes she could scream, wishes she could shout, "No," and that he'd listen, that he wouldn't try his luck atop the river. But onto the layered river the boy leaps, and sprints across, all two-hundred-plus feet at the slightest of angles.

Once on the eastern side, the boy slows eventually to a walk, either winded or bogged down by a sense of security. He then stops entirely. He turns around and holds his gaze with Reyn for only a few seconds, then is gone again, into a northeastern sprint, over the first of several yellow-green hills.

Reyn cranes her neck northeast, hoping the boy will come back into view. When he doesn't, she turns her attention to the blue mask still in her hand. The inside of the mask, formed to a small round nose, to undeveloped cheekbones, is white, save for a smear of red near the forehead. There is an indent an inch or so from the right eye, the impression no larger than what a grown man's thumb could make. Reyn flips the mask. The blue paint is uneven in spots, lighter around the jaws, nearer to purple on the chin, but for no obvious reason.

Go to the boat, Reyn thinks. *The boat can be your home.* She walks north, cradling the mask. *Drop the mask. Make the boat your home. Drop the mask. He'll find it. Drop the mask. Go to the boat. He'll find it. Drop the mask. Go to the boat. He'll find it. Drop the mask, go to the boat, he'll find it. Drop the mask, go to the boat, drop the mask, go to the boat, drop the mask, go-to-the-boat, go-to-the-boat, go-to-the-boat.*

Fifty yards later, Reyn stops. She looks again at the mask. She looks north. She looks northeast. *He had no weapon. He did not attack you. He is a boy.* A mangled boy, a scared boy, a boy who has been looking for something he'd lost. The thought, no matter how much she fights it, stays with her for another twenty yards or so, until, staring north once more, at the treeline, at the gravel, Reyn realizes that all she is walking towards, the only thing that lies ahead is the past. If she stays on course, if she sticks to what she knows, if she walks to that boat, she'll pass Vitri. He'll be there, on the forest floor, gasping for air. He'll be there, on the stump nearest that heap of charred wood. He'll be there, and there is nothing north without him, nothing to do but avoid him, walk west, travel around him, and for what—to watch him stare once more at the *American Queen*? She doesn't need that. No longer needs him. Refuses to let herself once more reach the point where she wishes the pain were still there.

Reyn approaches the river, long stick in hand. Where she figures the small boy sprinted across, she pokes aside the top layer of grass and weeds, revealing beneath it what appears to be a thin mound of wet clay. She inserts the end of her stick into the mass, then struggles to pull it free. She paces north and proceeds to fling more grass and weeds aside. Beneath is water. A current slowed by the clay—by a poor man's dam; by a young man's bridge. Reyn returns to where she'd first poked and removes more of the top layer, in all directions, until a four-by-four square reveals the mound to be just more than a foot wide and continuing northeast at an angle, the impressions of the sprinting boy's feet there but barely visible, barely felt.

After easing the blue mask into her backpack, Reyn tests just how much weight the clay can hold. Backpack on her shoulders, she steps atop and stands still. Within seconds she begins to sink. She steps off, tries again, but this time doing her best to hold the backpack to the side, arms shaking as she does so only seconds in. She sinks. She holds the backpack over her head. She sinks.

The boy is a magician. You are too heavy. You are incapable of running as fast. You will sink. You will take one misstep and fall. Your leg will be snared in a trap. You will drown.

Reyn walks backwards until her heels are within inches of the treeline. She keeps her eyes northeast. Acceptingly, Reyn sets the backpack on the ground, unzips its largest pocket, and begins plucking cans of food from the bottom. She tosses four of the seven on the gravel, knowing someone, or something, will find them, will find them all and put them to use, survive if only for a few days more. Three of five candles. One bottle of water.

Sacrifices she's willing to make if it means she's running toward hope, toward the chance to become someone new—herself. Because there's nothing here but shaping her life around pain. Around Vitri. And if not Vitri, around her mother. And around her father. Around the deepest cuts of loneliness. Those that occur when people held dear talk but refuse to listen.

Reyn zips the pocket. Stands up. Pulls the straps over her shoulder. Takes one deep breath. Two. Pictures handing this mask over to that boy, the joy that will come with letting him know that he was heard. And then Reyn takes off. She keeps her weight as forward as she can without toppling over, maintains an intense focus on her line, and leaps over the water that filled in her trial-run footprints, until she is sprinting atop the clay, across the river.

For fifty-plus feet she sprints, relentlessly, arms pumping with both violence and grace, springing off of her toes. Ten more feet. Ten more, ten more. And then she loses it. Her right foot slips. Her left knee slams into the clay. She falls, taking with her into the water the topmost layer of grass and weeds and twigs.

Panic. She kicks her feet. Loose grass flings every which way. She digs her fingers into the clay, peeling away chunks, shoving the mound further into the water, allowing a slow current to begin in the middle of the river.

Reyn feels that ball forming in her chest, forcing its way to her throat. *Forward*, she thinks. *Forward, forward, forward*, and, whether or not the ball makes its way off her tongue, Reyn crawls her way along the clay toward the eastern shore. *Forward, forward, forward*. Fifty feet from shore. *Forward, forward, forward*—Forty.

When she does, she is up to her thighs in soggy grass, what water she'd soaked up along the way returning itself to the river. And, standing there, her weight taking her and the clay an inch or so lower, Reyn allows herself to smile. She looks back across the river, at the shore, at where she began and thinks it so far away now. She can even see where she fell, evident by the current that continued to flow, carrying with it what its hands could grasp. With a sense of pride, she turns around and steps toward the shore. Twenty feet remaining. Fifteen. Ten, the riverfloor ascending, her steps along with it, knees high, feet down, water splashing around her. And then she feels it—some sort of hiss across her right calf. A snap in the water. She looks down, sees nothing but brown. But there is a sting in her leg, a growing sting, a throbbing sting.

Once ashore, Reyn takes off the backpack and lies down on the gravel. With the amount of water that had soaked into her clothes, Reyn struggles to roll up her pant leg, grimacing with each fold. There's a gash on the back of her calf. Two gashes. Three, the first short and shallow, the second deeper, longer, the third even more so. All three bleed onto the stones beneath her.

Immediately, Reyn reaches for her backpack. Lying on her side, she unzips the largest pocket and plunges her hand toward the bottom, searching for the bottle of rubbing alcohol. She pulls it out, twists off its top and pours more than she needs over her leg. Gasps—

—right pantleg still rolled, Reyn, past still in view across the river, gingerly walks northeast, toward sparse groupings of trees, into ankle-high grass. Clouds stir overhead as she stops and douses her calf once more with rubbing alcohol, thinned blood streaking to her damp socks—

—she passes an empty hunting shack, two of the four walls caved in, handfuls of bullet casings left behind. She walks over patches of uneven ground she assumes to be sites the blue-masked boys have dug and replaced as best they could, small footprints leading further northeast. Between two particular ridges, she spots two white-tailed deer, one buck, one doe, both sets of ears perked, their hair patchy but their frames, for the fifteen seconds they remain still, appearing as elegant as they should—

—her thighs and groin begin to burn. Beneath a young willow, she seeks shade, which, thus far, having walked entirely over gradual ridges and into the sun-fried valleys between, has been difficult to find. She sits against the trunk, her left leg flat on the burnt grass, the right crossed over to examine the gashes. Dry now, reduced to slivers of pink—

—sun high, hotter than it has been for days. No wind. Sweat, lots of sweat, lots of steps, lots of sweat seeping into her wounds, lots of steps burning her thighs. *Northeast, northeast*, past thicker clusters of trees—oaks and elms and sycamores—past thicker knots of weeds and brush, past doubt, past *they'll be just like the rest*, past shade, through hearty grass, over *maybe you should turn back*, eventually back into a valley as the sun continues to arc—

—*forward, forward, forward*, up the steepest incline Reyn has come across, struggling all the way to the top, breath heavy, toes digging. Young trees up to her chest, trunks the size of her ankles. High enough now to see just over the crest of the hill, Reyn watches smoke eddying into the sky. *Forward. Forward.* Once atop, she wipes the sweat from her forehead and looks down on a longhouse built from logs and in the process of being painted light blue, two of four sides complete. The smoke comes from its center, a narrow circle in the roof whose jagged edges impale risen ash. Leaning against the westernmost side of the longhouse is a bicycle. Small dark blue frame, white handlebars, white seat, its use evident when viewing the lawn, the narrow tire tracks around the house, up and down the slope, weaving beneath trees to the north that, through its sparse leaves, appears to have taut ropes strung from branch to branch.

Reyn, weight on her heels, walks down the slope, head up and scanning for any reason to turn back, or head west, eyes peeled for lurking masked, for steel traps, for rifles, for arrows, for everything that isn't there. Unable to completely combat the doubt, she raises her arms in the air as she walks toward the longhouse, surrendering before anything even begins.

Fifty yards. Closing. Arms: still in air. Mouth: dry. Sweat. The burn in her thighs easing, giving way to nervousness; flutters in her muscles. Twenty-five yards, on flat ground. A blue door, uneven logs as steps, bound by twine. Windows. Blue shutters. East of the trees: glimpses of green, shin-high corn stalks, the beginnings of what look to be caged tomato plants. She doesn't tell them to, but finds her arms dropping to her sides. Ten yards. The smell of food cooking. Meat. Fatty meat. Potatoes. Greens.

She approaches what she perceives to be the front door, and along the way catches a glimpse of flashing white and grey lights, of unknown characters inverted across windows. A sight Reyn tells herself is unreal. She thinks of McPHERSON's THEATRE, of the generator. Takes her backpack off and sets it on the ground. Again unzips the largest pocket, pulling from it the pen and notebook, pages partially dry, corners curled.

Reyn sets the notebook on the top step. She places the blue mask beside the notebook, eyeholes skyward, then reaches back in for the remaining cans of food, arranging all in a line on the bottom step and placing one candle atop, in the heart of which is carved R + V. With every intention to light the wick, Reyn pulls the book of matches from her pocket and, upon feeling the cardboard, understands that there is no point in trying, that it all will be too damp to ignite for some time. She backs away from the door and sits on the ground, pulling her knees to her chest. Hugs them tight. Curves her spine, rests her chin. Her eyes float from candle to door, from door to candle.

THE END

AUTHOR'S NOTE

To my mother, brother, and father, I am forever grateful—without your unconditional love and unending encouragement, wandering to the written word would certainly have been too daunting of a task.

To the friends that have investigated the industry just so that I wasn't left experiencing the highs and lows of the writer's journey alone, thank you. Your loyalty has meant so much to me.

I am deeply indebted to Caitlin Horrocks and Sean Prentiss, for their passion as instructors, their skill as editors, and also for their appetite as writers—each of you continue to inspire me.

Many thanks to the folks whose red pens have greatly impacted my work over time, including but not limited to different versions of *Wounded Tongue*. That's you, Daniel Abbott, and you, Alexandra Dailey, and you, Meghan McAfee, and you, Will Stefanski.

I especially want to thank you, Lindsy. Your love, patience, and intellect comfort and inspire me each and every day. You're the best.

And finally, to you, dear reader, I owe so much. Thank you for your time, and for making this fictional world spin.

Garrett Dennert obtained his B.A. in Creative Writing from Grand Valley State University, emphasizing in fiction and creative nonfiction. There, he contributed to the school's literary journal, *fishladder*, and soon after served as founding member and Nonfiction Editor of *Squalorly*.

Dennert has since been fortunate enough to place stories and essays at *Barely South Review*, *Midwestern Gothic*, *Monkeybicycle*, and *Whiskeypaper*.

Currently, Dennert calls Grand Rapids, Michigan home. *Wounded Tongue* is his first novel.

ORSON'S

EST. 2016

| www.orsonspublishing.com |

Made in the USA
Lexington, KY
28 April 2018